Zoe's Stories

A Romantic Comedy

Leah Hermann

Dedicated to my mom, who has always put her children first. The woman who took on the job of raising me when it could've been qualified as one of the most difficult tasks God has ever assigned, especially during those rebellious high school years. Thank you for teaching me how to love others as well as myself. Love you, Mom.

Acknowledgments

Special thanks to my sister-in-law, Patrisha, for your continued support—always the first one to share my posts and root me on. You always show interest in my writing, no matter what I decide to write, and it means the world to me.

Chi Hom, thanks again for another amazing cover. You are the Yoda of graphic design!

Another thank you to my editor, Liane Larocque, for sprucing up my manuscript. I value your input, and even more, your encouragement. Thank you for being an awesome editor!

The girls from high school and from my "ice cream" job, thank you for purchasing my novels. It hasn't been the easiest to gain a following, but your support has helped encourage me to keep writing.

To my husband, thank you for watching the kids when I want extra time to write and for sacrificing your relaxation time to read over my manuscripts.

Story One

I Want You Back

Chapter One

Three Types

Every guy wants that perfect girl.

Some guys look for a girl who lights up a crowd as soon as she enters a room. The type of woman who spends endless hours a week getting her hair and nails done. A woman who will endure one of those painful Brazilian wax jobs. You know, that kind of lady who draws in every set of eyes like a magnet. The girl who is responsible for wives becoming furious with jealousy due to their husbands' lustful stares at another woman—the kind of girl who is a certified trophy-wife.

Other guys want someone with brains—like Einstein's brain. Someone who can hold an intellectual conversation for hours. A partner who can "challenge" them. A woman whose beauty is shown through her thoughts and mind rather than physical means. She has a prestigious career and is raking in the dough—the kind of girl who is nothing less than a genius.

There are even guys who yearn for a girl who will take care of them, like my sister. The type of woman who can cook a three-course meal on a dime. A lady who will scrub a "blown up" toilet without complaint. Someone who will pop open that beer for her man without being asked. She's a professional dishwasher and does a load of laundry every other day—the kind of girl who will wait on her man hand and foot.

Guys don't ever give a girl like me a second glance. I'm just your average gal, who isn't anything special. Someone who spends a whole two minutes styling her hair in a side braid every day because her wavy, dirty blonde hair refuses to be tamed. A chick who forgets to shave more often than she's willing to admit. A woman who can have an interesting conversation but can't stand people who think they know everything—someone who likes to talk and laugh about silly, meaningless stuff. A girl who wishes she knew how to cook but whipping up a box of mac and cheese is the extent of her talent.

I am not a trophy-wife type of gal. I have an average IQ, and I could never be anything like my sister, who is Suzy Homemaker. I could never qualify as someone's "perfect" girl… or, at least, that's what I thought before Ethan came home.

This is the story of how I lost myself.

Chapter Two

Beach Bod

As I hold a dumbbell in each of my hands, I think I'm staring straight at one of *those* perfect girls guys yearn for. She looks like she has had her fat injected into all the right places—a real-life, curvy Barbie. Her body is perfectly tanned and toned. Her sports bra and cute leggings look like something straight out of a Victoria's Secret catalog. I don't think she's even breaking a sweat. There's not a hair out of place on her head, and she's been on the stair machine forever.

"Trophy-wife," I unconsciously say aloud.

"Earth to Zoe!" Lee shouts as he waves his hand in front of my face. "I told you, ten more reps. Let's go. I thought you wanted to get a beach bod for the summer?"

I stare at him, confused. "Oh, sorry. I was just thinking about something else and got distracted. What did you say?"

Lee places both of his hands on his hips just above his workout shorts. "I asked you if you want a bangin' bod for the summer or not?"

"Yeah, I do. I want abs like yours."

Lee lifts his shirt and pats his shredded stomach. "If you want these bad boys, you need to put in the work. You have to hit the gym more than just a couple of times a year and not live off fatty, processed foods."

"You know I can't go more than a week without a burger," I reply as my glasses start to slide down the bridge of my nose. "Push my glasses back up," I tell Lee.

He does as I instruct. "Now, start curling those dumbbells!" Lee demands.

"Ugh, my arms feel like jelly," I say as I struggle to finish my reps. "You know, everywhere else besides here and Florida, there's no such thing as a 'beach bod.' People who don't live on the coast don't even know that term."

"Oh, quit your whining, Zoe. There are so many people who would love to live in San Diego."

"I think I'm done for today," I say, exhausted.

"Seriously?" Lee crosses his arms in frustration. "You've been here a whole ten minutes."

I set the weights back on the rack. "You know I have work this afternoon, and my job is basically like a workout. Plus, I can ask you for a free training session any day."

Now Miss Barbie has made her way over to the treadmill and is running a marathon. She is like the Energizer Bunny, and I wonder if I had a trendy sports bra like hers, if it would give me a boost of motivation.

"Is that what you think of me? Your on-call professional trainer?" Lee asks with a hint of sarcasm.

Lee wasn't just my personal trainer who I took advantage of a whole two sessions out of the year, he has been my best friend since the first grade.

I remember the first time Lee and I met. It was during lunch. I was sitting on one of those long metal tables with built-in benches, and I was talking to a girl I just met a couple of days before. Lee walked up from behind us and wedged both of his hands between mine and my friend's shoulders. He forcefully pushed us apart like Moses parting the Red Sea and created a space between us for him to sit. I happened to already be on the end of the bench before Lee shoved me, so then half my butt was hanging off the edge. So rude.

"Excuse you," I said.

"Hi, ladies," Lee replied like a suave older man hitting on women at a bar.

At the time, Lee didn't look how he does now. No one would've guessed he would grow up and find a job in a gym. During our younger years, if I were to describe Lee in a nice way, he looked like he really enjoyed eating food, but if I were being blunt, I would describe Lee as a chubby sumo boy.

Also, Lee hadn't always had a fancy, slicked-back hairdo. Up until college, Lee's mom used to put a bowl over his head like a stencil to give him a haircut, or at least that's what it looked like. I guess it was typical of Asian moms to do that sort of thing, according to Lee. He said something about how his mom refused to pay a barber to do exactly what she could do for free. Apparently, Asians are pretty tight with their money, but nowadays, Lee doesn't opt for the "complimentary" family haircuts. Instead, Lee pays the big bucks to get his hair done. I give him continuous crap for spending more money on his hair products than me and *even* more crap for spending ten times as long as me to style his hair each morning.

Anyway, back to the story when I first met Lee during the first grade…

The girl I befriended ignored Lee and started to chit-chat with a different classmate who sat on the other side of her. I sat by Lee, uncomfortable and annoyed, and tried to hurriedly finish eating my PB&J.

"Zoe, I just came by to say hi," Lee said nonchalantly.

I didn't respond and continued to give Lee the cold shoulder. I contemplated moving over to a different table since I realized Lee wanted to make small talk, but as soon as he unzipped his lunchbox, I changed my mind. I caught a whiff of the aroma coming from his food, and I couldn't help but curiously glance over. I watched as Lee happily unwrapped a round, white bread ball. My mouth began to water when I saw him take a heaping bite. I wiped a little bit of drool off that was forming at the corner of my mouth as Lee looked over at me. He tore the bun in half and held out the food like it was a friendship offering.

"You want some?" he asked with his mouth full.

I eagerly nodded and set the sandwich on my paper bag. I anxiously grabbed the food out of Lee's hand and shoved the entire portion of bun into my mouth. My eyes lit up.

"Good, huh?" Lee said.

"Mmm! Best food I've ever had," I replied.

"You'd be a good opponent if we ever play chubby bunny," Lee chuckled.

"What was that?" I asked, delighted by the bun I inhaled. "And where did you get it?"

"It's called bao. My mom made them." Lee smiled for a second, and then his head dropped to his chest like he was disappointed. "Mark and Sophia made fun of me because they thought my lunch smelled weird. They told me my food smelled like salty garbage. It's not like my mom packed me stinky tofu."

"Is that why you came over to say hi? To find a better table to sit at?" I asked.

"Yeah," Lee responded.

I felt bad. Some of the kids made fun of my glasses, so I could sympathize with the chubby Asian boy.

The next day, Lee didn't have to wedge himself between another person and me. Instead, I saved him a seat, and to my surprise, Lee had his mom pack an extra pork bun so I could have one too.

Ever since then, we've been inseparable.

Chapter Three

The Housewife

"Yay!" Ashley shouts after moving her game piece. "Ice cream!"

"This game is for babies," Travis whines and crosses his arms.

"Aw, don't be such a poor sport, Travis. Your sister loves Candyland," I tell my nephew. "And I know for a fact that you do too. Are you just pouty because you aren't winning anymore?" I chuckle at Travis, but he just gives me a pouty lip.

"She always lands on the ice cream spot," Travis mumbles to himself.

Besides being a part-time dog walker, I also babysit my sister's kids, so she and her husband can have a date night every now and then. Oh, what I meant to say is, I babysit my *younger* sister's kiddos. Yeah… Trish got married right out of high school. She was swept up by my now brother-in-law, Roy, who has always been and still is kind of a deadbeat.

Although I should give Roy some credit—he was smart enough to put a ring on Trish's finger before someone else swooped her up, and I will say, Roy does make decent money, which allows my sister to stay home with the kids, but Trish puts in her hours too. So, I guess I refer to Roy as a deadbeat because he doesn't do crap around the house and makes Trish take care of the kids twenty-four-seven.

Anyway, Trish and Roy had Travis about a year after getting married. Travis was an "accident," if you believe in such a thing. I think everything happens for a reason, and I couldn't imagine life without my nephew. So, after they had Travis, Ashley came along two years later, and ever since then, my mom can't stop herself from reminding me that Trish is five years younger than I am, and number three is on the way. My mom always jokes about how I will have to freeze my eggs if I wait any longer to find a man. Yeah… my mom makes me feel fantastic about where I'm at in life.

"We're home!" Trish yells while walking through the door. She runs up to Ashley and Travis and gives them a big smooch on their cheeks. "How were my babies?"

"Just as easy as ever," I say.

"Ah, playing some Candyland?" Roy asks and plops down on the couch. Trish quickly walks to the kitchen to fetch a beer before Roy can kick his legs up on the recliner. "I'm beat," Roy says, which I find hard to believe.

It's not like he had worked today, and like I mentioned previously, I know Roy doesn't do anything around the house or watch the kids. I would bet my entire savings—which isn't much. It probably could buy you an outing to the movies, but that's beside the point. The point is, I would bet money that Roy was probably sitting on the couch all day before taking Trish out to dinner. So, what could he possibly be tired from?

"Here you go, baby," Trish says to Roy, handing him a chilled beer.

Roy didn't thank her. Apparently, he just expects a beverage to be placed in his hand as soon as he sits down.

When I first realized Trish's job consisted of being a server as well as a maid, chef, and so much more, I fumed.

"Oh, Zoe, don't give yourself an aneurism," Trish said.

"Are you kidding me?" I asked angrily. "Roy can change Travis' diaper once in a while, especially if you're in the middle of cooking or doing something else. You take care of the entire house by yourself. It's ridiculous."

She shrugged like it was no big deal. "It's my job. Roy goes to work and pays the bills. I knew this was how it was going to be even before we were married."

"Whatever. Just don't turn into Mom, okay?" I said, annoyed.

Trish shook her head. "How dare you say that. I'm nothing like Mom, and I take care of my kids."

"That's not what I meant…"

"You'll understand one day when you find a man," she replied. "Things change when you find that special someone. You end up making sacrifices you never thought you would."

At that moment, I felt like I was Trish's younger sister, and she was trying to give *me* sisterly advice.

I still don't understand Trish's reasoning, and I never will. I vowed to never let a guy take advantage of me the same way Trish lets Roy. I always thought of marriage and raising children as a team effort, even if one of the parents is able to stay at home. Trish is the perfect housewife, but I know she's not the only one who is a "stay-at-home slave," and I'm smart enough to know Roy isn't the only guy who looks for a perfect housewife. Since she's not the only one, maybe Trish had a point. Maybe my outlook on being a housewife would be different if I ever found someone to love me back. Who knows?

Chapter Four

Friends and Fro-yo

"Bruce, Zoe is here!" Mrs. Smith, Lee's mom, yells. "Come inside. I made some soup," she says, inviting me into her house. Mrs. Smith waves, urging me to follow her into the kitchen. "I also made bao. You should take some home. Bruce doesn't like to eat them like he used to. You know how he is with his no-carb diets." Lee's mom shakes her head in disapproval.

I guess now would be a good time to tell you that Lee's real name is actually Bruce. His first name is Bruce, and his middle name is Lee—named after the famous martial artist. Supposedly, Bruce Lee was Lee's dad's idol growing up.

Shortly after becoming friends and learning about the reason behind his name, I told him he didn't look like a Bruce, and I wanted to call him Lee. I told him if he let me call him Lee, I would be his best friend for life, but no one else was allowed to do so. Such a silly pact, but over two decades have passed, and Lee has continued to keep his word.

And since we are on the subject of names, I bet you are wondering how Lee's last name could possibly be Smith since it's not a very "Asian" last name. Well, it's simple, Lee is only half Chinese. His dad is Caucasian.

Lee's mom told me she knew her parents wanted her to marry an Asian man, but she argued she wasn't in control over the cards being dealt in her life. Mrs. Smith never passes up an opportunity to remind me how she and Lee's dad met.

Mrs. Smith always starts off the story the same way.

"All my friends would give me a hard time. They would tell me I was addicted to gambling and needed to stop going to the casino so often, but the only thing I found addicting was the sexy table games dealer—not that I was stalking him or anything. It's not like I memorized his work schedule. Mr. Smith was always placed at the Baccarat table, which happens to be my favorite game. I can't help it if that's what fate decided," Lee's mom says.

Mrs. Smith also likes to tell me how she would wear her nicest pair of earrings and jade bracelet. I kind of like hearing the story of how they met because it's sweet that the woman pursued the man for a change, and it's like a romantic love story being played on repeat.

Although I will say, I am thankful Mrs. Smith only mentioned it once—how she was obsessed with Mr. Smith's chest and arm hair, but I guess that makes sense why she's attracted to Caucasian men. Asian men have less body hair than I do.

Anyway, that's also why Lee is so tall. Full Asian men rarely break the 5'9" mark. I mean, Lee could've been the next Yao Ming, but basketball was never his thing.

Lee's pretty lucky though, he gets the best of both cultures. Most of the time, Mrs. Smith serves up delicious Chinese food, but some days, Lee's dad craves the typical American pizza or hamburger. Lee's mom always prefers to go to Las Vegas for vacations to satiate her love of gambling, but Lee's dad would rather go beach camping, or any camping at all, really. So, as far back as I can remember, the Smiths have always taken twice the amount of vacations compared to what a typical family would take each year.

"Hey, Zoe. You ready to head out?" Lee asks as he jogs down the stairs.

"Zoe's just about to have some soup," Lee's mom shouts.

I've learned to always go to Lee's house on an empty stomach and to never have anything planned within an hour of arriving. It's kind of like going to my own personal Chinese restaurant.

"Yeah, of course," Lee says as he walks into the kitchen.

"You need to eat too," Mrs. Smith insists. She places two bowls at the table, and Lee joins me. "You're nothing but skin and bones," Mrs. Smith says like she preferred how Lee looked during his younger years.

"Ooo, quail eggs," I say excitedly and clap my hands.

Lee's mom smiles at my compliment.

Lee's mom is also the perfect housewife like my sister, but she is also like the mom I never had.

When I was seven, I remember my dad standing at the front door with his suitcases. He told me he was going on a long trip, but that was a lie. Luckily, Trish was only three, so she doesn't remember anything.

I sat by the window on the weekends, wondering when he would come back, and every day after school, I hoped to see his car parked in the driveway. Every day was a disappointment, and it wasn't until three years after, I understood my dad wasn't on a prolonged vacation. I eventually realized he was never going to read me my favorite bedtime story again or tuck me into bed.

My mom cried for a month straight after my dad walked out. I thought it couldn't get any worse, but I was wrong. I never saw my mom cry again. You'd think that was a good thing, but it wasn't. It was like my mom shut down, and instead of sitting on the bathroom floor sobbing, she turned all her emotions off. Instead of hiding under the blankets and staying in bed all day, she made it a priority to go to Pilates six days out of the week. She ended up getting a full-time job at a bakery so she could afford the place we were living in and learned how to make different types of pastries and other goodies—probably thought she could catch herself a good man with those types of skills.

Then six months after, my mom started dating Dan, a guy she met through speed dating.

My mom continued her normal exercise routine and worked her usual forty hours a week, but now that she had a boyfriend who came over on his weekends, she spent all her extra time scrubbing the house from top to bottom to put on a "good show" for Dan. She didn't have any time for Trish and me. We were transferred to the bottom of her list of priorities. As a result, Trish spent a lot of time at our aunt's house, and I spent almost every day at Lee's.

Just before Trish graduated high school, Dan asked my mom to marry him, and eventually, they moved to Death Valley. I couldn't believe my mom agreed to live in the Devil's butthole. She could barely stand the summer weather in San Diego. Even though my mom is less than six hours away, she doesn't bother to get together in person during the holidays. We have our three-times-a-year facetime sessions set in place—my birthday, Thanksgiving, and Christmas. Trish has more sessions with Mom because hers includes Travis' and Ashely's birthdays.

I can't fully blame my mom for being absent throughout my childhood, though. Something in her snapped when my dad left. At least she isn't lonely anymore.

After my second bowl of soup, my stomach is filled to the brim, and I know I'm allowed to excuse myself. "Thank you for lunch," I say to Lee's mom.

"Don't forget your bao," she reminds me and hands me a bag filled with a dozen pork buns.

I smile warmly at her, and Lee and I head out the door.

Then, we stop by our local fro-yo shop like we do religiously every week, and after that, we head over to my place to watch some movies.

"I don't understand how you can still be team Edward," Lee says as we sit on my couch eating our yogurt.

I angrily point at the television. "I don't understand how you can *still* be team Jacob!" I shout, annoyed.

"It makes no sense. Bella could have a normal life with Jacob," Lee argues.

"Who wants a normal life anyway?" I counter. "And... wait, how is it 'normal' being with a werewolf? There's a high possibility Jacob could shred Bella's face to pieces, and all because he loses his temper. How is that *normal*?"

"Honestly, what I really don't understand is why we are binge-watching these movies again for the third time this year," Lee mentions. "And why do we have the same argument every time? Also, you are probably the only one on the planet who is still gawking over these movies."

I gasp, extremely offended by Lee's comment. "I am not the only person! Don't even go there."

"Okay, then name one other person you know who is still into it," Lee demands.

"That's easy. You."

Lee crosses his arms over his stomach and falls back onto the couch. He laughs hysterically like I've cracked a joke, and I glare at him because nothing I said was supposed to be funny. I get the feeling he is mocking me.

Once Lee catches his breath, he replies, "I hate to break it to you, but I only watch lame vampire romances because you are my best friend, and best friends make sacrifices for one another."

I desperately want to wipe that silly smirk off Lee's face.

"Oh, please. You know you enjoy watching *Twilight* just as much as I do. You just won't admit it. Seriously, one of these days, I will convince you to convert to team Edward," I say confidently.

"Yeah, that will never happen," Lee replies.

"Well, if that's the case, I guess we will be watching *Twilight* until I die." I nudge his arm with mine, half playfully and half frustratedly.

"So, I never asked how your facetime meeting went with your mom last week," Lee mentions. "I must've been too distracted throwing you a kick-ass birthday party." He smirks.

"It was pretty—"

"Hold that thought. I have to drop a deuce," Lee interrupts and rushes to the bathroom.

"Oh, my gosh!" I shout. "Do you have to do that every time?"

"Do what?" he yells.

"Announce you have to go number two," I say loudly from the couch.

"Oh, lighten up, Zoe. I let you know so you can guestimate how long I will be gone for."

I roll my eyes. "It doesn't even matter. Why do I need to know a time frame? I think you just like to announce it to the world."

"Don't you remember that one time I didn't tell you? You kept rushing me, asking me how much longer I would be every ten seconds."

"That was the first time we were watching *Twilight* since we'd seen it in theatres!" I shout, annoyed. "It was *one* time."

"Anyway, about that party. It was awesome, right?" Lee asks.

"It was an amazing party," I reply.

Really, my birthday bash only consisted of the two of us, Lee's mom and dad, and my sister's family. Lee rented one of those bounce houses for Travis and Ashley. For the majority of the party, we sat around in Lee's parent's backyard and ate food, which is what I prefer anyway. I like to keep it low-key and spend it with the most important people in my life.

"Oh, so tell me about how it went with your mom," Lee mentions again.

"You know… talking to my mom is always the same."

"Made you feel shitty again?" Lee asks, still on the toilet.

"Yup! How'd you guess? And speaking of shitty… don't forget to double flush."

"You are like a Nazi—the toilet Nazi," Lee says, mocking me.

"You know, my grandma used to have a Great Dane. The dog's name was Biscuit, and it used to take the most massive dumps. I would know because I used to shovel that poop for pocket money."

"I know, you've told me this already," Lee yells, annoyed.

"Yeah, but did I tell you that you would really give Biscuit a run for her money. You know, if you were to compare sizes."

"Compare sizes?" Lee asks, confused. "What do you mean by compare sizes?"

"Head out of the gutter, Lee. We are talking about defecating, not body parts. Plus, Biscuit was a girl, remember?"

"Oh, right," Lee replies.

"Anyway, you know I don't like seeing residual doo-doo in the toilet, and it makes the bathroom stink. So, make sure you double flush!"

"Yes, ma'am," Lee says, in a soldier type of voice, and I bet he saluted to the bathroom wall just now.

Back to the subject about my facetime session with my mom. Like I said before, I only talk to my mom three times a year. Last week was my birthday, and we talked for a whole nine minutes. Somehow, my mom always finds a way to make me feel crummy about my job, my goals, and pretty much life in general.

"Maybe I should start looking for a better job," I tell Lee, thinking of my mom's disappointment.

"What are you talking about?" Lee asks. "Don't let your mom get to you. Every time you talk to her, you think you need to change something. My parents don't care if I live with them for another twenty years, and that's how all parents should think. They let me live my life."

"That's such an Asian thing," I scoff. "We already went over this, remember? I said it depends on the kid. Some children would take advantage of staying at home with Mommy and Daddy. They don't learn how to be adults because they are mooching off their parents, and then you said that's how families create wealth by supporting each other and something about how it creates a strong family bond and whatever else."

Most Asian families couldn't care less if their kids lived at home their entire life. I can't relate. As soon as my mom got engaged, she kept trying to urge Trish and me out of the house to make room for her fiancé, and once they got married and decided to move to the desert, Trish and I sought out and rented the studio I'm currently in.

I was lucky enough to find a wealthy client with three dogs, so I could afford the rent by myself after Trish moved out. Between babysitting and dog walking, I was able to make ends meet. I wasn't raking in the dough or anything, and it sure would've been nice to have more support like Lee's family provides. Instead of spending his money on rent, which is crazy in San Diego, by the way… Lee gets to save almost his entire paycheck, and who knows what he's saving up for. I would assume his own place, but Lee seems content living with his parents. I always thought it would be kind of cool if he started up his own gym.

"Yeah, I know," Lee says, walking out of the bathroom. "But you know how my mom wanted me to become a dentist like my Uncle Ed. Lately, she's been more understanding about my job choice. Although, she's always been good about showing her support either way."

"That's good," I reply, becoming distracted by the movie.

It's the part where Jacob convinces Bella to kiss him. Man, that kissing scene is fire! Secretly, I wondered what it would be like in real life for two men to love me like Jacob and Edward love Bella. Heck, I wondered what it would be like for *one* man to love me.

Chapter Five

Genius Wife and Fate

"Sorry, Zoe, I don't know where I put Kiki's harness. I must've misplaced it the other day when I took her to the vet," Susan says as she hands me one of Toby's old collars. "Hopefully, this will do until I have time to get another one for her."

"Um, okay. I will make the collar as small as I can," I say.

"Thanks a ton, Zoe!" Susan pulls her keys out of her designer handbag. "I have to get going. I'm running a little late today, but I left your check on the kitchen counter. I added a little bonus," she mentions while winking at me.

"You didn't have to do that, Susan."

"I wanted to. You take such good care of my babies. I don't think I could trust anyone else with them."

Susan is one of those "genius wives" I was talking about. She's the CEO of one of the biggest medical supply chains in the world. She works all hours of the day, just like her husband who is an attorney. I'm not sure why Susan and her husband, Raymond, decided to get three dogs. They don't have any time for fur babies with their busy work schedules, let alone each other.

One time, Susan asked me for a favor.

"I know it's not listed in your job title, but do you think you would be able to stay over a few nights next month and watch my babies?" Susan asked me before rushing off to work. "Raymond planned us a getaway for our anniversary, and we don't see each other much these days."

Susan seemed excited as she thought about spending some quality time with Raymond. She's one of the sweetest ladies I had ever worked for, so I was glad I could help her out. Plus, my bank account needed a little boost.

"Of course," I said.

Susan and Raymond's return flight home ended up landing later than expected, and I fell asleep on their couch. I awoke to the two of them "whisper arguing" while they were walking through the door, but I pretended to still be asleep.

"Well, frankly, I find it a little deceiving you haven't been taking your birth control," Raymond said angrily.

"Well, frankly, *I* find it hurtful that you want to wait another five years before we try to conceive," Susan countered.

"I made it clear before we got married that I wanted to put our careers first before having a child," Raymond snapped back. "This shouldn't come as a surprise to you."

I continued to act like I was sleeping. I wondered if I should yawn obnoxiously, pretending I just woke up and hadn't heard a thing.

The argument continued, and Susan said, "We have put our careers before everything else, and now I think it's time for us to consider starting a family."

Raymond scoffed. "The next thing you will have me consider is letting you stay at home with the baby and sacrificing your position with your company."

"I love my job, and I don't plan on quitting, but if you want to bring up that subject, there's more to life than work," Susan replied. "When you are on your deathbed, and there's one last breath in your lungs, you aren't going to be thinking about how you should've put more hours in at work."

The dogs began barking at something outside, and I decided it was the best time to "wake up" and roll off the couch.

"Oh, hi. I didn't even hear you guys come home," I lied, sitting up straight and stretching my arms above my head. I even added a little yawn to my theatrics.

I was surprised Raymond, being an attorney and all, didn't have a better closing argument. Susan sure won that case, hands down. I guess that's what Raymond gets for marrying a woman with big brains.

"Come here, Kiki!" I shout, and the miniature poodle makes her way over to me. Susan heads out the door as I buckle the collar onto Kiki's neck. It fits, but it's also a tad loose. I scratch Kiki behind her ears and look at the collar, debating if I should go ahead with Susan's directions. "Toby's big bulldog neck isn't exactly the smallest, is it?" I say to Kiki.

After staring at the collar for a solid minute, I decide it might be okay. I mean, Susan is the one who made the suggestion in the first place. I wrangle up all three of the dogs and begin our walk around the neighborhood toward the local park. I try to keep Kiki's leash pulled in an upward position, so she doesn't slip her head through the collar. I wouldn't have a job if Kiki ran off, or even worse, got hit by a car.

As we stroll through the pathway in the park, I become distracted by some boy who is riding his scooter. He isn't paying attention to his surroundings and is coming straight for us. I try to push the dogs onto the grass to the left of me so the kid can pass without colliding with us. In the process of moving aside, I accidentally allow Kiki's leash to fall below my hip, and the tension in it relaxes. Kiki takes advantage of my mistake, quickly wiggles her head out of the collar, and runs to chase a leaf across the park.

"No, Kiki! Come back!" I shout, but she is fixated on the leaf being blown along the grass.

I try to yank the other two dogs toward Kiki, but now Toby and Rocky are trying to sniff something and are pulling in the opposite direction of where I want them to go. I look around frantically and try to decide if there's someplace I can tie down the two dogs while I rescue Kiki, but there's nothing nearby—just a really wide palm tree the leashes wouldn't fit around.

"Oh, my gosh! Susan is going to murder me!" I shout and grab the leashes with both my hands. I try to yank the dogs in the right direction like Santa lugging a heavy sack. I'm slowly inching closer to Kiki, but the wind is blowing the leaf closer to the street. "Kiki!" I yell again, panicking. I put my entire body weight into each pull and lean forward, causing my glasses to fall onto the ground. "Please, God. Don't take Kiki!" I pray aloud as I watch Kiki follow the leaf into the street through my blurred vision.

A car swerves around Kiki, and finally, my prayers are answered. I see a guy sprint into the street and scoop Kiki out of harm's way. I take a deep breath, and my heart stops racing.

Kiki's hero jogs toward me with the miniature poodle in his arms, and as he gets closer, I begin to voice my gratitude, "Oh, thank you so, so much. I can't believe that happened."

"No problem. I think it happens more often than people would imagine. I'm glad I was in the right place at the right time, but you should really consider investing in a harness for your dog. It would help prevent another scare," our savior replies.

"I feel so terrible, like an irresponsible dog walker," I mention and pick my glasses off the ground to wipe them clean on the bottom of my shirt. "Yeah, Kiki's not my dog. But I guess I shouldn't have—" I place my glasses back onto my face and look at the man standing in front of me—"oh, my gosh! Ethan?" I say, surprised.

"Hi, Zoe. Long time," he says, grinning.

"Oh, my gosh! Ethan." I clear my throat. "Sorry, I already said that," I reply awkwardly. "What I meant to say is… wow, it's so good to see you! Like, *really good*."

I try to hug Ethan and hold my arms up, but then I remember I have the dog leashes in my hands which makes it nearly impossible to wrap my arms around him, and Ethan's still holding Kiki, so I slowly lower my arms, embarrassed.

I continue to ramble uncomfortably and say, "I thought you were still living up North after graduating from Stanford. I can't believe you made it into Stanford.

That's not what I meant to say. Um, I mean, I can. It's just such a prestigious school and all."

I instantly regretted saying that. I hate to admit that I occasionally stalked my ex-high school sweetheart on social media. And when I say occasionally, I mean monthly or maybe more… for the past decade. Every time I looked on Ethan's social media page, I hoped for an updated picture of him. Secretly, I wished he had gotten fat or had to wear a toupee to cover his receding hairline, so I would feel better about him dumping me, but Ethan only ever posted random pics of his company's robots because he scored an awesome job as a lead scientist at some artificial intelligence company.

I know you are probably thinking I'm such a savage for wishing that upon someone, but it's not like I made a creepy voodoo doll that looked like Ethan and stabbed it with a bunch of needles.

Ethan and I dated for six months, two days, ten hours, and seven minutes, back when we were in high school. All right, so I guess Ethan doesn't *actually* qualify as my high school sweetheart, but those were the best days of my life!

I remember Ethan taking me out to the movies. We only ever caught glimpses of the film since the real reason we went to the theatre was so we could suck face for two hours. Ethan was also the first guy who stuck his tongue in my mouth, in case you were wondering.

"I'm still living in Northern California. I'm just in town for another week," Ethan replies.

"Well, it's so good to see you." Why can't I stop repeating myself? "Uh, you look really great."

Ethan did look really great—nothing like he did in high school. He had quite the pizza face back then, but apparently, that's not a problem for Ethan anymore, and rather than putting on weight, Ethan looks like he's gotten more fit. There's also no wig or lack of hair. Now, Ethan reminds me of a swoonier Josh Hutcherson with his mysterious but welcoming eyes, beautiful brunette hair, and strong jawline.

"You haven't changed one bit," Ethan says.

I run my hand down my side braid and realize Ethan is right, which makes me feel self-conscious. I haven't changed, not one bit, and I think Ethan might consider this as a negative thing.

So, that brings me back to the topic of Ethan crushing my heart. One day, Ethan had just decided he didn't love me anymore, and yeah, he said it to my face. So heartless. Oh, so I said Ethan "*decided* he didn't love me anymore" because just the day before Ethan broke up with me, I read an article in one of my magazines. It said love isn't just a feeling but also a choice, which makes sense. It's a choice to stay loyal to your significant other, and it's a choice to show them how much you care with various gestures. It's a choice not to walk out on your family and abandon them.

Anyway, I guess Ethan had gotten tired of loving me. Maybe I was a difficult person to love for a prolonged period, or maybe Ethan thought his time was better spent elsewhere, like with his "bros" or anyone else, for that matter. Either way, I wasn't worth loving, and it's not like he was the first guy in my life to leave me.

"So, what brings you to town?" I ask.

"Well, I had to make time to come to our high school reunion this weekend," he explains. "I thought it would also be a good excuse to spend time with family."

I hadn't the slightest idea about any details regarding a high school reunion.

"Oh, yeah. I was thinking about going too," I lie.

"You know, we should get some lunch tomorrow and catch up," Ethan suggests.

My palms begin to sweat with happiness, and my heart pounds even faster than when Kiki ran into the street.

He continues, "It's been too—"

I can't contain my feelings wanting to burst out of my body. "YES! I'd love to!" I shout, interrupting Ethan.

"Oh, uh. All right. Cool," Ethan says, taken back by my enthusiasm. "I've been dying for some Mexican food. It's not the same where I live."

"I bet," I say, grinning ear to ear.

"Let's go to that one restaurant by the beach. They have the best carne asada."

"Anywhere you want to go," I say. I would meet Ethan in the filthiest gas station bathroom if he asked me to.

"Anyway, I'd better get back to reading my work e-mails. They like to pile up when I'm not at the office." Ethan hands me Kiki. "Better hold on to that one."

I nod and continue to smile. "Kay."

"I'll see you at noon?" Ethan asks.

"Noon is perfect!" I answer an octave too high.

"All right. See you then," he replies before turning to walk back toward the park bench.

I wave awkwardly at Ethan's backside. I cannot wait for my date with Ethan tomorrow!

Chapter Six

Model Date

Ethan said I looked the same as I did in high school, so as I stand in front of my bathroom mirror, I slowly pull my side braid out, allowing it to unravel. I don't want to look ordinary or mediocre for Ethan. I want him to want me. I want him to decide to love me again.

I know what you're thinking—why the hell are you going to lunch with Ethan after he broke your heart? Why give that jerk the time of day? There are other guys more worthy of your attention. Zoe, don't do it!

While your opinion might be true, I can't help how I feel, and it's been such a long time since high school. When Ethan broke up with me, I wasn't done loving him. Plus, I couldn't possibly hold a grudge for twelve years.

Lee told me his grandma used to always tell him that holding a grudge is like holding a match between your fingertips. As it burns hotter, you will eventually only end up hurting yourself. I think it was an old Chinese proverb or something.

I arrive at the restaurant and notice Ethan already has a table. I eagerly wave at him as I walk nearer, and then out of nowhere, someone sits in my chair. I pause mid-walk and linger a couple of feet away from the table, confused. Who just sat down with Ethan?

"Ethan! I thought that was you. I almost didn't recognize you," says the girl sitting in my seat. "What are you doing here?"

"Hi, Noelle. What a pleasant surprise," Ethan replies.

Now I realize the seat-jacker is Noelle, as in, prom queen Noelle. As in the most popular girl in high school, who was voted most likely to become famous.

"Oh, my gosh, wait. Ethan, are you here for the high school reunion this weekend?" Noelle says in her annoying high-pitched voice.

"Yes," Ethan responds.

"I knew it!" Noelle says and makes little annoying baby claps with her hands underneath her chin. "Seriously, Ethan. You look so good. What are you doing these days?"

"Not too much. I've just been swamped with work."

"Oh, yeah!" Noelle says happily. "I heard something about you becoming super successful from working on robots and whatever." Noelle leans in toward Ethan, pulls her perfectly straightened amber hair to one side, and shoots him a sultry smile. "I've been in the modeling industry for the last ten years. I've made a pretty good living, but probably not as good as you. The word gets around when you start making six figures. Anywho, not sure if you saw me on the cover of—"

Noelle is ruining my chance with Ethan! I know I should do something fast. I don't know where I ended up finding some courage, but I walk up to the table and interrupt. "Hey, Ethan!" I say.

Noelle leans her back into her chair and looks at me like she's disgusted at my presence. "Oh… Zoe?" Noelle asks. "Oh, my gosh. Zoe! Wow, you have not changed one bit."

I wish everyone would stop saying that. I guess letting my hair down wasn't enough to make a difference in my appearance.

"Hi, Noelle," I say flatly.

Noelle laughs like I said something funny. "*Cute* T-shirt," she says. "And those look like the same glasses you wore in high school. I guess some things never go out of style."

Noelle's sarcasm isn't subtle at all.

"Thanks," I reply, unable to think of a comeback. After all, Noelle is perfect. Not sure how anyone could come up with anything negative to say about her.

Noelle begins to laugh even harder at my response, and blood rushes to my cheeks.

I chuckle uncomfortably to myself. "Not everyone can afford designer clothes," I say quietly.

I instantly realize I just took a jab at myself, and I probably should've just stayed silent, but it's hard for me to do that when I feel out of place—the most awkward comments escape my mouth when I'm in uncomfortable situations.

Noelle props her head against her elbow that's on the table and continues to stare hard at my clothes, amused. "I can see that," she replies while smirking.

Thankfully, Ethan finally decides to join in and saves me from Noelle's harsh judgment. "Uh, Noelle. Zoe and I were going to have lunch," Ethan says.

"Oh…" Noelle looks confused for a second. "Well, excuse me," she says. "I didn't mean to interrupt your, um… *date.*"

"It's not a date. We're just catching up," Ethan replies.

Noelle smiles at me like she was happy to hear that from Ethan and turns to him and says, "That's good to hear because I may want you to take me on a date before you leave town." Noelle winks at Ethan.

Ethan clears his throat and covers his smile behind his hand. I can't believe Ethan said this isn't a date. How could I be so stupid?

Noelle scoots her chair away from the table, and as she stands, I notice Ethan's gaze follow along Noelle's perfect, size zero body. I think Ethan's undressing her with his eyes. No, I *know* for a fact he's imagining her in her birthday suit, but what guy in the restaurant isn't doing just that?

"Zoe, I really do like your glasses. So vintage," Noelle says, feistily but also jokingly, before walking away to join her table full of model friends.

I feel their glares on my back, and I wouldn't be surprised if Noelle was telling her stick-figure friends about my thrift store shirt. I will say, it makes me feel better to see the group of models only drinking skinny margaritas, and the one who is actually eating the burrito as big as her forearm will be vomiting it up later, I'm sure. It's a reminder that I'd rather be healthy instead of a twig and have to worry about counting calories.

"I guess everyone is craving Mexican food today," Ethan says as I take a seat.

I laugh nervously. "Yup."

"Your hair looks nice. I don't think I've ever seen it down before."

I smile. "So does yours."

Oops, that didn't make sense. I wish my nerves didn't get to me like they do.

"Uh, okay," Ethan says and runs his hand through his hair and chuckles at my comment. "I'm glad you had time to make it to lunch today."

"My schedule is pretty open these days," I admit.

"Anyway, tell me what's been going on in your life since high school," Ethan says.

"Not much. Just walking dogs. They are pretty great. Their names are Kiki, Rocky, and Toby. You know… in case you were wondering, and Kiki was the one that got away yesterday. Um, in case you forgot."

Man, I bet Ethan thinks I'm a bore. I wouldn't be surprised if he wasn't impressed by my lack of career. Also, I should probably stop rambling.

Ethan laughs. "Oh, yeah. Kiki made it home safely?"

"She did. I held her the *entire* way."

"Good to hear, and don't feel like you did anything wrong. You looked like you were beating yourself over Kiki's leash slip. Just last month, Anna told me her dog accidentally fell into her pool, and it drowned."

"Oh, no. That's terrible," I reply. Wait, is Anna someone Ethan's seeing up North? Yeah… that is really terrible.

"Tell me about it, but accidents happen all the time."

"Is Anna your, um… is she your—" I stammer.

"Yeah, Anna's amazing."

I feel my body sink deeper into the chair. I want to lift the napkin I placed on my lap and hold it in front of my face, so I can disappear while Ethan talks highly about his girlfriend.

"She really knows how to make a man happy."

Maybe I can excuse myself for a potty break.

"She was a hot commodity, but lucky for me, I was able to acquire her services," Ethan adds.

Hold on a minute. Now she sounds more like a hooker rather than a girlfriend.

I finally chime in, "So, you're not dating Anna?"

Ethan chuckles, "What? No! She's my housekeeper. Although, maybe, I should've given Anna a chance since the last girl I dated told me she didn't believe in settling down or commitment. I doubt Anna would've been interested, though. I don't think she's into men twenty years younger than her."

Holy cow, Ethan really had me worried there. "So, you had to cut your last girlfriend loose because she didn't believe in marriage?" I ask, thankful Ethan is a bachelor.

"Yeah, can't get those eleven months back. Uh, so, that reminds me. I wanted to tell you that I feel like a dirtbag for dumping you the way I did."

I shrug. "It's no big deal," I lie.

"I know how upset you were."

I shake my head. "I wasn't upset. I got over you in a week or so." Another obvious lie.

Ethan glares at me. I think he can see through my façade.

"Fine!" I exclaim. "I didn't get over you within a few days! Yeah, I was really sad."

"I'm sorry, Zoe. I was young and didn't care about people's feelings. I wish I hadn't been so harsh."

"It was a long time ago," I mention. "Let's not bring up old memories."

Or better yet, let's not bring up *bad* memories.

"Yeah, I guess you're right," Ethan agrees and changes the subject. "It's nice to see a familiar face when I come to visit. Over the years, I've lost touch with a lot of my high school friends. Work has just consumed my life, and everyone's off getting married and starting a family."

Ugh, don't remind me. Don't remind me of successful careers and babies. My mom does enough of that. I'd rather talk about other things on our date—I mean, at lunch… I'd rather talk about other things during *lunch.*

I don't want to just be friends with Ethan, and I can't help but wonder if I looked anything like Noelle, if Ethan would've considered this a date. If I knew how to flirt like Noelle, would Ethan want me? I bet he wouldn't be able to take his eyes off me if I wasn't just ordinary Zoe.

"I understand," I reply. "Maybe we can hang out at the reunion for a little too."

"I would love that," Ethan says, but then he looks over at the group of models again, and Noelle gives him a little wave.

Within the last minute, I made the executive decision to go to the high school reunion. I bet Lee knows all the details. I just have to convince Lee to go. It might be my last chance to see Ethan before he leaves.

Chapter Seven

New Me

"There are three days until the high school reunion," I say to Lee as I finish running on the treadmill.

"Okay… and?" he asks, confused.

"Well, I need a training session tomorrow and the day after," I reply firmly.

"I don't understand," Lee says. "What does that have to do with the high school reunion?"

"I want to lose three pounds before Saturday."

Lee scrunches his head between both his hands. He does this when I frustrate him. "You can't just lose three pounds in three days, Zoe. Not unless you starve yourself, and that's not even real weight-loss."

"Please, Lee. I need this."

Lee pauses for a second and looks at my puppy dog eyes staring back at him. "Fine. Let's go over to the squat rack," he sighs. "But just for the record, you are being ridiculous."

I ignore Lee's comments. "And you are coming with me on Saturday."

"No way," Lee responds.

"Come on!" I plead. "I need you there for support."

"I thought we already made up our minds. The last twelve years, you've been telling me you didn't care about seeing any of your old classmates. You said it would just be another popularity gig like it was throughout high school."

"Well, that was until I bumped into Ethan the other day," I explain as I position myself under the squat bar.

"Ethan?"

"Yup! He looks so good."

"You mean, pizza-face Ethan?"

"His face has cleared up. Ethan's more like a yummy cheese pizza now rather than the pepperoni and sausage type. I think I can get him to ask me out on a real date before he leaves town. I just have to make a better impression on him when I see him at the reunion."

"So, losing three pounds is going to make Ethan want to ask you out on a date?" Lee asks skeptically.

"No, not just that. I'm going to buy myself a nice outfit. I was also thinking about getting my hair and makeup done."

"What's wrong with your hair?" Lee asks, confused as he looks at my braid.

"I just don't want it to look the same as it always does," I reply hesitantly.

"Hmm. Okay, whatever makes you happy, I guess."

"So, you have to go with me. Plus, you know you want to show off your hot bod. No one will know what hit them when you flex those guns."

Lee looks at himself in the mirror and speaks to his reflection. "You got that right, baby." Lee flexes his bicep and kisses the top of his muscle.

"And you think I'm ridiculous? You're *clearly* the ridiculous one—doing weird things in front of the mirror," I laugh. "Now, how many squats do you want, coach? I'm ready to put in the work."

"Wow, Zoe. I've never seen this side of you before."

"It's the new me."

Chapter Eight

Pretty Woman

"I want to look like a model," I say to my hairdresser before she styles my hair.

"That's new," Aaliyah responds, surprised. She isn't used to my high maintenance demands. I usually only get my hair cut twice a year, and I always request the same boring style. "Special event tonight?"

"High school reunion," I reply.

"Ooo, that *is* special. Where's it at?"

"It's at some fancy restaurant by the beach. I guess the invite said formal... so, just trying to follow the dress code," I add nonchalantly.

"Mmhmm, I see..." Aaliyah pauses for a brief second and squints hard at my reflection. She places her hand on her hip. "Girl, you can't fool me. I know what you are really saying—you're *saying* someone special is going to be there. Someone *important*."

I awkwardly chuckle, realizing I couldn't play off why I needed a new look. "How'd you know?" I ask.

"Comes with the job, and you wanting me to do your makeup too was also a pretty good clue. So, tell me, who's the lucky guy? Is he a fling from the past?"

"Yeah, Ethan."

Aaliyah gasps and pauses from her work. "*The* Ethan? Ethan who broke your heart? Ethan who told you he didn't love you? *The same* Ethan who doesn't deserve a minute more of your time?" She puckers her lips, which tells me she is bothered by my answer.

"Uh… maybe," I reply hesitantly.

Aaliyah places her hand on her hip again and continues to look at me, annoyed. "Mmhmm," she says. "I cannot believe you want to try to seduce that no-good-boy."

"He's really not all that bad," I try to convince her. "Plus, it's been such a long time since high school. We went to lunch the other day. Ethan apologized for dumping me the way he did in high school, and everything seemed pretty chill."

"No, no, girl. Don't do it. Sounds like trouble to me. I told you I would hook you up with my cousin Justin. He's a much safer bet."

"Aaliyah, please don't make it harder for me than it already is. You know how I have a difficult time with my confidence and meeting people, and I already told you, it would never work out with your cousin. I don't want to be forced to watch football every single weekend. It's not my thing. Justin would probably tell everyone I'm lame because I'm clueless about the game. I know the person who throws the ball is called the Quarterback, and that's pretty much the extent of my knowledge of football. Plus, I'm a terrible cook. Justin would probably ask me to make chili for him during the game, and then he would be all disappointed when I pour some canned stuff into a crockpot and call it a day."

Aaliyah sighs. "I'm sorry. I always say things I shouldn't. I'm surprised I keep clients as long as I do," she laughs. "And I don't blame you. I heard my cousin has become addicted. He doesn't just watch his favorite team—he watches *every* game they air."

"See. I just can't wrap my head around that," I reply, not sure how someone can be that obsessive, but then I remember my *Twilight* fixation and feel like a hypocrite.

"Oh, I know, girl. Anyway, I'm here to help any way I can," Aaliyah mentions.

"And I'm grateful because I wouldn't know where to start," I admit.

She smiles and winks at me. "Don't you worry. You will have Ethan falling at your feet once I'm done with you." She waves her comb in a circle above her head for dramatic effect. "You will be like a serene goddess. He won't know what to do with himself."

I hope what Aaliyah said is true. I hope Ethan will want to do more than just eat lunch with me.

"You and your husband have been together for a long time. I don't think you ever mentioned how you guys met," I say.

"Oh, I haven't told you how we met? Well, funny story," Aaliyah says. "We met through mutual friends. It was one of my best girlfriend's birthdays, and we were all hanging out at a bar to celebrate. Kirk came over and tried so hard to flirt with me. He had all these ridiculous jokes up his sleeve and the craziest pickup lines."

"What did he say?" I ask.

"Girl, I don't even know. It was forever ago, and Kirk was making no sense half the time he was talking. He was a nervous wreck. I think he might've said something about me being a cat and spending nine lives with me. He cracked me up."

"So, what else happened?"

"Well, he rambled on the whole night, but no guy had ever tried so hard to get me to go on a date with him. I thought, if this guy is willing to convince me for two hours straight, I ought to give him a chance, and I'm sure glad I did. That man treats me like I'm the rarest gem on Earth."

"You're so lucky," I say.

"You know it, girl, but now take a look," Aaliyah says as she spins my chair around, so I can look at myself in the mirror. "Now you are ready to make Ethan fall to his knees. He will be begging for you the moment he lays eyes on you."

I don't look anything like myself. I run my fingers through my straightened hair. It's no longer a frizzy mess. Instead, it's smooth and silky, and I feel like a luscious mermaid with long flowy locks. My face reminds me of a celebrity walking the red carpet at the Grammys, and I feel amazing.

I *could* be a goddess. You could call me Aphrodite.

Next on my list is to pick up a jaw-dropping outfit. Half of my wardrobe consists of old worn-out high school clothes, and the other half—purchased at the local thrift store. You'd be surprised by the quality of clothes you are able to buy on a budget.

Anyway, I walk into Marcus and Co., which I heard carries nice dresses. I honestly can't remember the last time I've worn a dress—oh, yeah… my mom's wedding when she married Dan, and I had to be her maid of honor.

She picked out the most frilly, disgusting-looking dress for me to parade around in. I looked like one of those vintage dolls being consumed by endless ruffles. Luckily, it was a small gathering, so I only had to deal with a few family members "fake complimenting" my hideous outfit.

And speaking of ugly dresses, the store I've walked into doesn't have any hideous ones on its racks, and within less than a minute of entering through the doors, I spot the most gorgeous dress, and I instantly gravitate toward it like Kiki does with leaves blowing across the park.

But before I remove the dress from the rack, I glance at the price tag. $550.00… and discounted? I feel like someone has just punched me in the solar plex, causing me to gasp for air. That's more than what I spend in a single year on clothes… or possibly a decade.

"Is there anything I can help you find?" the sales lady asks. I notice her nametag reads Vivian.

"Uh, yeah. I mean, no, I'm good. Thanks."

As I am just about to turn and make my way out of the store, Vivian quickly pulls the dress off the rack that I was eyeing a minute ago and says, "This dress would look perfect on you."

"It's really beautiful," I say. "But, um, I can't—"

"You should try it on," she insists.

"Oh, I don't know about that. I—"

"Come on. I will put this in the fitting room for you right now," she says, and without my consent, she heads toward the rooms.

I don't protest and follow her. I've always had a hard time saying no to people, and apparently, still do.

I really hate that quality about myself. Trish says I let people walk all over me, which is somewhat true, but I can't help it. My mom wasn't the greatest female role model, but luckily for me, my best friend never takes advantage of my weakness, so most of my life, it's not an issue.

I slide my baggy shirt and jean shorts off and slowly step into the black lacy dress. I slide the straps over my shoulders and look up at myself in the mirror.

"Oh, wow," I say to my reflection.

"Let's see it," the sales lady says. Vivian is impatiently waiting outside my fitting room, and I wonder if that's part of her job. "Come on out."

I hesitantly unlock the door. Vivian places her hands over her mouth and gasps at the sight of me.

"It does fit you perfectly. I think this dress was made for you."

"You think so?" I ask, becoming excited.

"You look amazing, like a model. Do you like it?"

I like the compliments, even if it was coming from a middle-aged woman who was getting paid to feed me kind words.

"I love it," I reply. "It's nothing like I've ever worn."

"Okay, perfect!" Vivian shouts, clasping her hands together. "I will meet you at the register as soon as you're ready."

"Um… all right," I stutter and walk back into the dressing room.

I stare at the stranger in the fitting room mirror for a second time. I like how she looks. She's not timid. She doesn't lack confidence. The unfamiliar girl I'm looking at isn't average. She's someone every guy wants, and that's when I decided I *need* the dress if I want to be Ethan's girl.

Chapter Nine

So Damn Hot

I pull up to the restaurant in my janky beetle. I notice Lee leaning against the driver's side of his car, and he's dressed in a nice suit.

As soon as I step out of my car, Lee yells, "What in the world happened to you? I don't think I would've recognized you if it weren't for that bright yellow turd you're driving."

"Hey!" I shout back. "This yellow *turd* has driven your butt plenty of places! So, don't diss the bug."

Lee chuckles, holds his elbow out to escort me toward the restaurant, and says, "You know I'm just messing around. You look great." But then he can't help himself from cracking another joke. "Although I would've gone with the classic side braid if I were you. It hides the… less flattering side of your face much better."

I pull my hand away from his arm, give him an intense glare, and shove him with both my hands with all my strength.

Lee laughs. "Better hit the gym a little harder if you want to start a fight."

"You are the worst," I say, and Lee wraps his arm around my shoulders.

"I know." Lee squeezes me tightly. "And I have to admit, I don't know if I like you without glasses."

"I don't either," I reply. "These over-the-counter contacts are irritating the crap out of my eyes."

Lee removes his arm as we walk through the restaurant doors and into a private room overlooking the ocean. It feels like there are hundreds of people, but I instantly scan the room for Ethan.

"Looks like your man is chatting it up with what's her face, over by the bar," Lee says as we continue to linger by the doors.

"What should I do, Lee?" I ask, panicking.

"Uh… well, for a start, you could go say hi," he suggests. Lee shakes his head because he thinks I'm acting ridiculous.

"I don't know if that's a good idea. Noelle is a monster. She's a real-life vampire who drains every ounce of confidence from your body. Maybe it would be better if I wait until Ethan moves on from her or until she needs to use the bathroom. I don't do well with blood-sucking demons."

"Okay, Twilight, whatever you say. I'm gonna hit the buffet. You want to stand here all night and stare at Ethan like a stalker, or you want to get some food?"

"I'm coming," I say and follow Lee, but not without glancing over my shoulder a few times to get a glimpse at Ethan and Noelle. I could get an opening any minute.

As we stand in line, I hear a voice coming from behind us.

"Oh, don't tell me! Bruce is that you?" an old classmate of ours yells.

Lee and I turn around. Lee forces a smile and unenthusiastically waves. "Hey, Margo. How's it going?" he asks.

Margo is overly excited. She was the captain of the dance team in high school. I usually don't use the word "cocky" to describe girls, but the word seems to fit Margo pretty well. I heard she wouldn't allow certain body types on the team, and if I remember correctly, I think she spread a rumor about Lee and me being friends with benefits or some similar nonsense.

"Wow, Bruce!" Margo says, twirling a strand of hair between her fingers. "You look A-mazing! Just amazing!"

Lee smooths his slicked-back hair. "Uh… thanks," he says and looks at me with wide eyes, and we both turn forward and grab a plate.

I can read Lee's mind. He's thinking how Margo's voice is annoying because she sounds like she's talking through her nose. Lee knows Margo would have never given him the time of day back in high school. She was always too good for everyone, but now that Lee has shed some pounds, she's interested.

I also think I remember seeing Margo post something on social media about her husband leaving her for her younger sister. Margo seems like she's on the prowl tonight, and she wants to have Lee for dinner.

I have to admit, she does look pretty good. Maybe Lee should just go for it. He hasn't been with anyone in years.

As we scoot down the buffet table, Margo continues to chat it up with Lee. I wish I had gone before him, so I didn't have to deal with Margo leaning across me while she conversed with Lee.

"Tell me what your secret is, Bruce. Your arms look massive. You're like an Asian Arnold Schwarzenegger," Margo giggles.

She's making me uncomfortable, but Lee is probably more so. "Thanks, Margo," Lee replies quietly.

I try to push Lee down the line a little faster, but it's pointless because other bodies are holding us up. I think about ducking out early, but I look at my plate and realize I only have a roll and butter.

"Tell me more about what's been going on with you, Bruce. You aren't seeing anyone, are you?" Margo asks and purses her lips as she looks at me.

"Um, Lee and I are just friends," I say.

"Oh, phew!" Margo says. "I mean, that's too bad. I thought for sure you two were going to get married after high school."

As we approach the end of the buffet line, Margo quickly walks around me and grabs Lee by the hand. "Come on, we have some catching up to do. It's been, like, forever and a half," she giggles.

Lee looks over his shoulder. He looks mortified as Margo continues to pull him over to a table, which reminds me of a crocodile dragging its prey into the water.

Now, I'm friendless at the reunion, and I stand awkwardly looking for a place to sit.

"Hey, you!" I hear a voice and realize Ethan is walking toward me. "Wow, you are a sight for sore eyes."

I try to suppress my excitement. "You too—uh, I mean, I meant to say, you don't look too shabby yourself."

"Meh, I look all right, but you. Wow!" Ethan says. "All the guys here can't keep their eyes off you. I had to hunt you down when I heard a few of the guys talking about how gorgeous you look tonight."

I feel my face become warm due to Ethan's flattery.

"I had to get to you before someone else did," he mentions and realizes I'm holding a full plate of food. "Oh, sorry. Let's find a place for us to sit down so you can enjoy your dinner."

Ethan places his hand on the small of my back and guides me to a table. My palms become sweaty from all the excitement. The endless workouts I overcame the last few days have paid off. My hair and makeup got Ethan's attention just like I hoped, and my dress has made me the talk of the reunion.

Ethan pulls a chair out for me. "You sure do look beautiful tonight," Ethan says.

I smile and realize I've barely said anything in the last couple of minutes. We had already talked about our jobs when we had lunch the other day, and it turned out Ethan didn't just land a great career working with AI, he owns the company. I wondered how I could've possibly missed that detail when stalking him on his social media page.

Anyway, we even talked about how our families were doing, and now I'm having a hard time finding the right words to start a conversation. For a moment, I think about quoting a flirtatious line from *Twilight* but abruptly decide against it.

Surprisingly, I'm feeling pretty confident, and I think of how Aaliyah mentioned Kirk's jokes and one-liners and say, "You know how people mention Disneyland is the happiest place on Earth?"

"Uh, yeah…" Ethan says, confused—unaware of where I'm going with the conversation.

"Well, I guess no one's spent a night with you."

"Huh?" Ethan asks. "Oh! Oh!" He finally starts to laugh, but I think it's a fake laugh. "I almost forgot how funny you are, Zoe."

I start to feel my cheeks become rosy again. "Dumb joke," I mumble to myself and look down at my plate.

I become more embarrassed thinking about how the joke could mean more than just watching a movie or spending an innocent night together. I didn't realize until now that it could be qualified as a dirty pick-up line.

"I liked your joke," Ethan says and then grabs my hand from across the table.

I look up and grin. "Really?"

Ethan nods his head. "I also almost forgot how much I enjoyed spending time with you. We should have dinner tomorrow night before I leave to go home."

"Yes!" I shout too loudly, but then I think back to Ethan telling Noelle our lunch hangout wasn't a date, and all of a sudden, I feel less enthused.

"Can I pick you up at five?" Ethan asks.

Now he would just be leading me on if he wasn't asking me on a date, but I shouldn't get my hopes up.

"Of course," I reply. "Where did you want to go?"

"It's a surprise," Ethan smirks.

"Oh… okay," I say skeptically.

"It's a date."

My posture abruptly straightens, and my eyes widen. "A date?" I ask.

Ethan chuckles to himself. "Yes. You look so…"

"So what?" I ask anxiously and allow my excitement to escape its containment box inside my chest.

Ethan rubs his forehead like he doesn't want to admit something. "My mind keeps saying you look so hot tonight, but I know girls don't like hearing that. I already told you, you look beautiful and mentioned how all the guys are saying how gorgeous you look. You are leaving me speechless tonight, which doesn't happen all too often."

Ethan begins slowly rubbing his thumb back and forth across the top of my hand, and his touch sends goosebumps crawling up my arm.

"I don't mind," I say.

"You don't mind what?"

"I don't mind you telling me I look hot."

I know, I know, most girls would *not* be okay with that compliment, but I've never had anyone acknowledge how I look… at least not in a positive light. I've always been that "Plain Jane" type of girl. Guys never used the words beautiful or gorgeous when referring to me. No one ever talked about my outfit unless they were making fun of my favorite tie-dye shirt I wore once a week since my sophomore year of high school.

"In fact, you should keep the compliments coming," I joke, but I am kind of serious.

Ethan laughs. "I can do that," he says in a swoony voice. He leans closer. "You know, I was actually thinking we should go to the movies before I take you out to dinner. I always thought you were a good kiss—"

Out of nowhere, Lee plops himself into the empty chair beside me, which causes him to ram into my chair and interrupt Ethan and me. Ethan removes his hand that was on top of mine, taken back by Lee's intrusion.

"Ugh! Lee!" I shout angrily and glare at him.

"Sorry to interrupt you guys, but you see that mob over there?" Lee asks me as he nods his head toward the group of girls sitting at a table.

"Uh… yeah," I reply, annoyed. "What about it?"

"Well, the mob keeps getting bigger and bigger. Some of them keep touching my shoulders and arms. One of them told me I looked like the statue of David… at least what she could see, and then she looked straight at my junk. I don't even remember that girl from high school. I feel so violated."

"Huh?" I ask, confused. "Oh, you mean that naked statue by Michelangelo?"

"Yeah, but that's not the point! They won't stop talking about my muscles, and well, you know, and I think I'm getting a migraine from Margo. Her voice is causing permanent ringing in my head," Lee says.

I look at Ethan and see he's scrolling through his phone, and I'm thankful Ethan is distracted.

"Holy cow, Lee," I angrily whisper. "You didn't have to come over right this second to tell me this. I'm kind of in the middle of something… *important*."

"I told the girls you have IBS, and I needed to make sure you are doing okay," Lee responds.

"IBS?"

"Irritable bowel syndrome. I told them I've never known anyone with as sensitive of a stomach as yours. As soon as food goes in, it comes out."

I glance at Ethan again. Luckily, he is still busy with something on his phone.

"What the hell, Lee?" I ask, frustrated. "So, are you telling me they probably think I'm going to shit my pants on the way home?"

"It's a possibility," Lee laughs.

"Did I ever tell you how much I hate you?"

"Yes, all the time."

"Sorry, guys," Ethan says, tucking his phone into his pocket. "There's actually an urgent e-mail I should've replied to earlier, but I need to get to my laptop to send some information. I must have missed it when I scanned through my inbox this afternoon." Ethan looks at the time on his watch. "It's already getting late, so I think I will call it a night." Ethan stands, and I become even more furious at Lee's poor timing. "I can't wait to see you tomorrow, Zoe." Ethan smiles at me and waves at Lee.

As soon as Ethan turns his back to exit the room, I slap Lee on his shoulder.

"So weak," Lee says jokingly. "All right, can we go now?"

"I guess!" I yell.

"Well, I don't want you to have an accident in the middle of the restaurant," Lee says sarcastically.

I roll my eyes. "You are so annoying," I reply.

"Well, at least you got what you came here for, didn't you?" Lee asks. "If I heard correctly, Ethan said you guys have something planned for tomorrow."

My scowl changes to an overjoyed expression after being reminded about my date tomorrow. "Can you believe it?" I ask excitedly.

"Does that mean you are bailing on fro-yo?"

I place my hand on my forehead because I can't believe I double booked. "I totally forgot!"

"It's fine," Lee says, but he does sound kind of disappointed.

"We can go earlier, like, in the afternoon instead," I suggest.

"I have sessions all morning and afternoon tomorrow."

"I can bring some fro-yo by during one of your breaks."

"Better not. I will look like a hypocrite if my clients see me snacking on frozen yogurt when I'm always telling them they need to stick to a strict diet."

"Rain check?" I ask, feeling terrible for letting our fro-yo date slip my mind.

"Yeah," Lee replies. "But only if we leave now."

We look over at the "mob" table and notice Margo is waving Lee back over. Lee looks back at me like a terrified child who has just watched his first horror movie. I nod, and we book it out of there.

Chapter Ten

Prom Date

After spending an entire paycheck on that fancy designer dress for the reunion, I ended up borrowing one of Trish's dresses to wear to dinner with Ethan. Unlike me, my sister didn't shop at the thrift store.

I took one of Trish's dresses that's made of spandex or some type of stretchy material because her boobs are three sizes bigger than mine. If someone took a picture of just my chest and posted it all over the internet, no one would be offended or say a word because they would just assume it was a photo of a boy's body. All right, I guess I wouldn't go that far, but you get what I'm saying. I have no boobs!

Anyway, earlier this morning, I went and purchased a straightener and the cheapest makeup I could find. I replayed a YouTube video of a makeup tutorial five times before attempting wing eyeliner. I poked myself in the eyeball two times with the end of the mascara wand before I was satisfied with my eyelashes. I ended up passing on the blush because I couldn't figure out how to make my cheeks look less like Pikachu's and more like Julia Robert's in that one movie—after she gave up being a hooker. I also opted for the uncomfortable contacts. I decide that once my finances recover from my dress purchase, I will invest in better ones—preferably ones that won't completely ruin my eyes.

I don't want to leave my date with Ethan to chance. This is the only opportunity I see in my future—the opportunity for me *not* to be single for the rest of my life.

I convinced myself that spending all day getting ready for my date was not a complete waste of time, and I'm kind of glad Lee was busy at the gym. I needed every minute of the day to get ready. I doubt I could've spared two hours to get yogurt with Lee today, so I'm glad I didn't have to squeeze that into my schedule.

Ethan is right on time—not a minute late. I quickly look in the mirror one last time to make sure I look satisfactory before answering the door. I'm not put together quite as well as I was for the reunion, but I'm pretty confident I look far from ordinary.

"Hello there, beautiful," Ethan says.

I grin widely and write off my long day of primping as a success. "Hey," I say, trying my best to hide my excitement, and then I remember I should compliment him too. That's what adults usually do when they go on dates, right? "Anyone ever tell you that you don't look like the usual AI Engineer?"

I lock the door behind us, and Ethan asks, "What is someone with my work title supposed to look like?"

"Uh, I was just trying to say you look nice too, but um, I guess I always pictured people who work with techie stuff to be unattractive… or balding… someone who wears a toupee or has a receding hairline… or something along those lines."

Ethan has a good laugh as we walk to his car. "Oh, so you are saying I'm required to be *ugly* if I want to work with artificial intelligence?"

I shake my head as Ethan opens the door for me. "Like I said, I was attempting to give you a compliment," I explain again. "I was trying to say you look more like a swoony lawyer rather than a geeky guy who's into robots." I feel like I'm digging myself into a hole. "You know what? Let's just forget I made those comments about the hair loss stuff."

"Ah, all right. It's not a big deal. I guess I'm glad you think I look like a sexy lawyer you can't wait to put your hands all over," Ethan says happily, and I'm relieved he wasn't offended by my strange compliment.

We arrive at the restaurant, and Ethan asks, "So, I bet you are surprised?"

I nod my head, concealing my true thoughts. Ethan had chosen the restaurant he had taken me to before the winter formal dance during high school. I could never forget the place because it looks like a lighthouse and because Ethan paid more attention to his friends that night than me—his date.

I remember playing it off the whole time like I wasn't angry Ethan didn't give me any attention. I didn't want to ruin our special night out. I guess Ethan really believed in that saying, "bros before hoes" or whatever.

When I went to vent to Lee about my night with Ethan, he just told me that's why he avoids all high school events. Lee said something about them being drama. While I was silently fuming at winter formal, Lee spent his time in his parents' garage "wrenching" on his car. That was Lee's extra-curricular activity in high school. Maybe I should've been smart like Lee and skipped the lame dances.

I try to suppress the memories of the night of winter formal as we are seated at the table.

"I thought the restaurant would bring back some old memories," Ethan says. "That was a nice night, wasn't it?"

I guess Ethan didn't remember the night like I remembered it. I nod and lie, "Mhmm."

For a portion of the night, Ethan talked about the project his company is currently working on. I understood a good amount of what he was trying to explain to me, and for the most part, I was able to stay attentive. I didn't want to seem like a total ditz, which might've been a turnoff. Thankfully, I was only distracted by Ethan's majestic eyes once or twice.

"So, anyway, enough about my boring job," Ethan says. "I've had such a fun time hanging out with you. I wish I could stay and visit longer."

"Me too," I reply.

"You know," Ethan says while grinning, "I'm planning on coming home again for the holidays. The big project my company is working on should be done before then, and I'm planning on spending time in San Diego for almost an entire month."

"That's awesome."

"Yes, but what I was going to say is that I think we should see each other again when I come home."

Underneath the table, I'm counting the months on my fingers, trying to figure out how long I will have to wait to see Ethan again. Three months is a while, but… wow! Ethan wants to see me again! My future status is looking less like "single" and more like… "ready to *mingle*," uh but ready to mingle only with Ethan.

"I would love, love, love that," I reply.

"That makes me happy to hear," Ethan says and relaxes back into his chair.

As we wait for our dessert, Ethan stares at me, and I become self-conscious.

"What?" I start to panic and hold my hand up to my face. "Do I have something hanging out of my nose?"

Ethan chuckles. "No, not at all."

"Then what?" I ask.

"Nothing," he replies but continues to keep me in his gaze. "I just can't believe how lucky I am to be sitting here with you."

I smile and bask in Ethan's words.

I wonder if he thinks I'm the perfect girl yet.

Chapter Eleven

On a Scale of One to Spicy

I hit the gym for another workout session with Lee.

"I seriously thought, in my entire life, I would never see you so motivated," Lee says and crosses his arms across his chest like he's trying to figure out my motives.

Or maybe he's more peeved rather than curious because he's had enough of being my free trainer.

"I told you, this is the new me," I say unevenly while panting heavily.

Lee grins before pushing the button on the treadmill, which increases the machine to a slight incline.

"Oh, believe me, I didn't forget," he says in a sarcastic tone.

I glare at my trainer, but not for making me run a thousand miles today. I realize Lee still isn't on board with all the changes I've been making, or maybe just the reasons why.

Lee ignores my death stare and asks, "So, how did your date with Ethan go?"

I answer by nodding my head and smile while trying to slow my breaths.

"What's that?" Lee asks. "I didn't hear anything."

"Good," I manage to reply. "He wants to see me again when he comes home for Christmas."

"Oh, does he now?" Lee pushes the button a second time, and now I'm really struggling to keep pace. "So, Mr. Ethan wants to give it another go, huh?"

I nod my head again, hopeful Lee will accept a nonverbal response this time.

"What did you say?" Lee asks.

"Yup," I reply, becoming annoyed Lee isn't acknowledging my head nods, and it's not like I'm training for an uphill marathon. This is ridiculous.

"What do you think made Ethan decide he wants you back?" Lee increases the incline a third time.

"Uh—" I say, but I'm too winded to continue with an explanation.

"Sorry, I couldn't hear you," Lee jokes, but in an angry tone. "Speak up, Zoe."

"I—hate—you," I say through my gasps for air.

Lee finally hits the off button, and my jelly-like legs step off the treadmill. I instantly plop myself onto my back.

"You should probably get off the floor before you get staph," Lee suggests. "A nasty skin infection will probably ruin your 'new' look, and we wouldn't want that, now, would we?"

"Can't you just accept this is who I am now?" I say, matching Lee's vibe. "Best friends aren't supposed to beat each other down—they are supposed to lift each other up."

Lee can see that he's pushing my buttons and begins to lay off a bit. "Sorry, you're right. What was I thinking? Let me *lift* you up," Lee says sarcastically and holds out his hand to help me up.

I slap his hand away and get up by myself. "Seriously, Lee. I think—no, I know for a fact that Ethan likes my new look. So, I don't understand why you don't."

"Well, beauty is in the eye of the beholder," Lee mentions. "It's not that I don't like your new look… I just don't love it."

"That's rude," I say, irritated.

"What? I liked your glasses and frizzy hair."

I roll my eyes in disbelief. "*Please*, no guy wants to date Mia from *The Princess Diaries*… before she gets her makeover. In fact, I'm actually considering saving up for a boob job."

My words have created a vortex, and Lee's glance is sucked directly to my chest. I quickly fold my arms over my boobs.

"Don't stare at them!" I shout.

"What? I can't help it. You brought it up!"

I keep my arms crossed. "Don't be such a guy," I reply.

Lee looks up, and I relax. "Your body is fine," Lee tries to reassure me.

"I know," I say. "That's the problem. My body is just… *fine*, and I don't want to be just fine. I want my body to be desirable and sexy."

Lee looks annoyed.

"Seriously, Lee!" I shout in frustration. "Okay, go ahead and rate me on a scale of one to ten."

Lee shakes his head. "No, I don't want to do that."

"Do it!" I demand. "I'm trying to prove my point."

"No."

"Please," I plead puffing out my bottom lip. "Please."

"No."

"Do it, and I won't make you watch *Twilight* again until next year."

Lee sighs, giving in. "I don't know, Zoe. I guess with your new look… I would say… a seven."

"That's it?" I ask, frustrated.

"Seven, point, five?" Lee says quietly like he's unsure if it's a good enough of an answer. "See! I knew this was a bad idea."

"Okay, whatever! So, you think I'm a seven, maybe slightly higher, but on a scale of one to ten, I want to be a solid ten like Eva Longoria. You know she's got all the curves," I say while outlining my body as if I actually had a booty and chest. "She's got junk in all the right places, and if I was more well-endowed, I would be a solid ten too."

"So, you too want… junk in all the right places?" Lee asks, squinting at me like I'm talking gibberish.

"I mean, yeah. I want to be spicy like Eva."

Lee scrunches his forehead between his hands. "Who are you, and what have you done with Zoe?"

Lee may not agree with the changes I've made, but I've never felt better. The old Zoe would have never been able to get Ethan back.

Chapter Twelve

Supernova

Two months have passed since Ethan returned to his home in Northern California, and since then, Ethan has made it a priority to call me every night before he goes to bed. And since we are on the topic of priorities, I guess I should mention I've made a few of my own. One—watch a new makeup tutorial on YouTube every other week. Two—when paying with cash, all the extra change goes into the "new boobs" jar. And three—hit the gym four times a week, if not more.

I wouldn't say Ethan and I are exclusive right this moment, but I think I can make that happen when he visits in December. I just have to keep my routine at the top of my list of priorities and never revert back to my old ways.

Lee still doesn't like when I straighten my hair—a reminder that I'm not the "same ol' Zoe" anymore, but once in a while, I will still rock the side braid. Although, I no longer allow my hair to be a frizzy mess. Lee rarely sees me in my glasses anymore since I've upgraded to prescription contacts. Also, I try not to mention Ethan too often in front of Lee because he gets annoyed easily when I bring up that subject, for whatever reason. I think Lee doesn't believe in long-distance relationships. So, he probably thinks I'm wasting my time, or maybe it's because I treat Lee like my girlfriend, expecting him to constantly lend an ear, but can you blame me? That's the role of a girl's best friend—a good listener.

I glance at the clock on the wall in my studio. Ethan should be calling me any minute. I turn off the T.V. and quickly walk to the bathroom to remove my avocado mask, but what do you know? As I am just about to wash off the green mush on my face, my phone rings. I think about scrubbing it off quickly but then decide not to. I don't want to miss Ethan's call. I sprint over to my phone. Facetime? I guess Ethan wants to facetime tonight, which is weird. He very rarely does that.

"Um, um," I say, panicking while trying to decide if I should press the green accept button on my phone or the red button.

I don't think Ethan will mind my mask. Okay, accept!

"Hey, there's my girl," Ethan says. He's looking away from the phone screen, probably finishing up something on his laptop. "I've been missing your voice."

I giggle into the phone. "Same here," I reply.

Ethan finishes up whatever he's doing on the side and glances at the phone screen. He looks shocked. "Oh, woah. You scared me for a second. For a moment, I thought I phoned that green monster from *Ghostbusters*," he chuckles uncomfortably.

"Sorry, I can wash it off if you don't mind waiting," I reply, embarrassed.

"You don't have to do that," he says. "I know what your beautiful face looks like underneath."

"I'm glad you haven't forgotten," I reply happily but regret answering the phone with no makeup, and even worse, with goo all over my face.

I vow to never let Ethan see me like this again. I know you probably think I'm being ridiculous, but I'd rather not be referred to as Slimer from *Ghostbusters.*

"So, anyway, have you checked your mail today?" Ethan asks.

I have a bad habit of tossing all my mail on the table. Usually, the pile accumulates for a solid two weeks before I get around to going through all my bills and whatnot.

"No," I respond. "Why do you ask?"

"I mailed you something. It was supposed to arrive this afternoon."

I anxiously walk over to my stack of mail and shuffle through it. "I found it," I say excitedly.

I flip it over to open it and realize Ethan had written a note on the sealed flap. It reads: *In case you receive this before I call you, don't open.*

"Okay, so am I allowed to open this now?" I ask impatiently.

"Yes, please. I want to see your reaction."

I rip that bad boy open with no hesitation and pull out a ticket.

"What's this?" I ask and realize what Ethan had sent me as soon as he begins to explain—an airline ticket.

"I couldn't wait until December to see you."

I'm speechless and don't know what to say.

"So… what do you think?" Ethan asks, unsure.

"Oh, sorry," I apologize. "I guess you can't see my super excited grin underneath all the avocado," I laugh.

"Ah, you had me worried for a moment. So, you think you can make it this next weekend?"

"Yes!" I exclaim.

"I can't wait," Ethan replies.

I mean… I'm sure Lee will understand if I need to miss our fro-yo date on Sunday. We can always reschedule for another day.

When I arrive at the airport, Ethan immediately greets me with a long fiery kiss—the kind where the guy runs his fingers through your hair, and you wonder where the moment would've led to if you were in a bedroom rather than in public.

"You look more beautiful than I remember," Ethan says.

I guess my hard work paid off. "You really know how to sweet talk a lady," I reply.

"I know you just got off the plane, but I have another surprise for you," Ethan tells me.

"Are you going to show me one of your freaky AI robots?" I joke.

Ethan chuckles. "No, that wouldn't be very romantic, would it?"

I have a feeling this is going to be an awesome weekend.

"I must be the luckiest girl on the planet," I say.

Ethan smirks and grabs my suitcase. "I hope you brought a bathing suit."

I hurriedly follow behind him and grab his hand. "You never mentioned anything about a bathing suit," I reply and look at the autumn leaves on the ground as we exit the airport building. "Isn't it kind of chilly for a swim?"

"Haven't you heard of a heated pool?" Ethan asks, tossing my suitcase in the backseat.

I assume that was a hint toward what my next surprise is, but I'm terrible at guessing. Does Ethan have a pool at his house? The only romantic thing I can think of that involves a pool is one of those floating buffet-type things resorts provide for honeymooners in Bali or the Maldives. I've done a lot of travel daydreaming through pages of magazines if you couldn't tell, but yeah… I didn't even think twice to pack a bathing suit, so I don't know what I'm going to do about that. What I did pack was waterproof makeup—glad I didn't forget those necessities.

"Where are we going?" I ask impatiently. I roll down my window and can smell the salt in the air.

"Just a short while longer," Ethan says.

"Are we going to your place?" I ask, hoping for another hint.

"No, but good try."

"Are we going to the beach?"

Ethan looks at me and shakes his head. "You aren't very good at guessing."

Finally, we pull into a parking lot to a resort. "What are you talking about?" I shout and point to the resort. "This is the beach."

"Correction. We are staying at a resort *by* the beach," Ethan says.

"Same—freaking—thing," I reply.

"I'm going to make this an unforgettable weekend," Ethan mentions.

I hope he does, I think to myself. If Ethan hadn't broken my heart in high school, he might've gotten more than just make-out sessions at the movies. Now that

Ethan's flown me Upstate and rented a room at a fancy resort… I might let him be my first.

YES! You heard me correctly. Please don't judge! I'm twenty-eight and have never made love to anyone. No one's ever wanted to lay me down and ride me long and hard. Who would want to make sweet love to an average-looking chick? My best friend rated me a seven and a half out of ten, but after the last couple of months of dedicating copious amounts of time and upgrading my appearance, I would hope most guys would say I'm at least a nine.

We finish checking in at the front desk, and as we begin to walk toward our room, Ethan says, "Close your eyes."

"What?" I ask, unsure of why I need to shut my eyes.

Ethan abruptly stops walking to the room. "I want you to close your eyes."

I let out an awkward chuckle. "But then I can't see where I'm going."

"That's the point," Ethan replies. "I will hold your hand." He smiles slyly.

"Oh, gosh. Okay," I say. I close my eyes and hold out my hand.

"Promise you won't peek," Ethan says.

"Scout's honor," I reply while giving him a half-salute.

Ethan guides me to the room, and I can hear him slide the key into the reader to unlock the door.

"Can I open my eyes now?" I ask impatiently.

"Not quite. I will let you know."

Ethan pulls me into the room. I feel my feet drag along the tile floor, and there's a hint of freshness and salt in the air—the kind of scents you can only inhale while being outdoors.

Ethan lets go of my hand. "Hold on. Give me one more minute. Keep your eyes shut."

A loud pop of a cork echoes in the room. "What are you doing?" I ask.

I finally hear Ethan's footsteps coming toward me. "You can open your eyes now."

I see Ethan standing in front of me. He's handing me a flute filled with champagne.

"Ooo, so fancy," I say and take the drink from his hand, but then I start to look around the room.

The room is massive and two stories. The beams on the ceiling consist of various beach woods, and the room is lined with ivory walls. There's an endless row of glass doors that are wide open, allowing the ocean breeze to seep into the room.

"Holy cow! This room looks almost exactly like the place Edward and Bella stayed at!" I shout excitedly. I quickly set my glass down at the nearest table and run around the room like a child hopped up on candy. "Oh, my gosh! This is so amazing! I mean, it's not the exact same, but close enough." I hurriedly make my way over to the glass doors and notice the beach is just past our little backyard area. "The ocean's a little farther away, but this pool is ridiculous!" I continue, "I've never had my own private pool at a hotel before. Now I don't have to worry about kids swimming in the same pool."

"Who are Edward and Bella?" Ethan asks.

I try not to sound too annoyed, "You know, from *Twilight*?"

"Sorry, I'm not familiar with—" Ethan replies. "Oh, wait, you're talking about the band *Twilight*. That's neat, I guess. Anyway, what was that about the kids?"

I turn toward him, shocked, and honestly, kind of offended. I cannot believe Ethan doesn't know who Bella and Edward are. Has he been living under a rock his entire life? I abruptly turn my gaze back to the pool and the distant ocean, so Ethan doesn't question me about the annoyed look on my face. I'm going to pretend like Ethan never said he hasn't heard of my all-time favorite movie.

"Uh, you know, because little kids pee in the pool," I explain.

Ethan chuckles and takes another sip of his champagne. "Hmm. All right. I guess you have a good point," he replies and walks over to me. "Are you hungry? Should I order us some room service?" Ethan stands beside me and wraps his arm around the back of my waist.

I look over at Ethan and turn my body toward his, so I can kiss him. Ethan has earned it.

Ethan pulls away so he can speak. "Should I take this as a no?"

"What?" I ask, looking into his lovely brown eyes.

"You aren't hungry?"

I place my hands on the back of his neck. "Oh, uh… well, I did eat a whole bag of peanuts while I was on the plane," I say.

Ethan smirks at my answer. "I think we should take a swim in the pool since you aren't ready for dinner just yet."

I continue to linger in Ethan's embrace. "But I didn't bring my bathing suit. Someone didn't tell me to pack one."

"That might have been intentional," Ethan replies. "I didn't pack mine either."

I breathe in deeply, excited but nervous at the same time. Even though Ethan and I have had multiple make-out sessions, I can't suppress my anxiety. I feel like if I get into that pool with Ethan, there would be nothing leading up to that "special moment"—stepping into the pool with Ethan meant I would be saying yes. It's so abrupt, but I also don't want to be a thirty-year-old virgin. I didn't expect Ethan to skip third base and just slide into home. I think about wearing my underwear and bra as a bathing suit but then remember I only packed enough for my stay.

Ethan tucks a strand of my hair behind my ear and says, "It'll be fun."

"Um, okay," I say hesitantly.

Ethan slouches down to look me in the eyes. "Zoe, you don't seem like you want to."

I take a step back, away from Ethan. "I do. I—I'm just a little nervous," I admit.

"We can do something else if you don't want."

I shake my head, thinking about how much I care for Ethan as well as, you know, the whole thirty-year-old virgin nightmare.

"No, I want to." I pull my shirt over the top of my head and try to focus on how hard I've been hitting the gym the last couple of months.

"You are absolutely the most beautiful woman I've ever laid eyes on," Ethan says.

I slide my shorts off, but Ethan continues to stare at me, still fully clothed. I hug my body and awkwardly glare at Ethan, hoping he will remove his shirt.

I'm confused, so I ask, "Are you going to—"

"Oh," Ethan chuckles. "Sorry." He finally sets down his glass of champagne. "I was just hypnotized for a moment there."

Suddenly, I start to feel my insecurities creep out of hiding as Ethan reveals more of his body to me. Ethan wouldn't win any body-building competitions, but he's toned from head to toe. His abs are rock hard, just like his—

"Zoe, are you okay?"

"Oh, um. Yeah," I reply. I swallow deeply. "Do you think you could close your eyes until I get into the pool?" I ask.

Ethan looks at me questionably. "Uh… of course. Just let me get in first. It's a little chilly standing out here naked."

Ethan steps into the pool and turns away from me. I wonder what my first time will be like. I gather some courage and finish undressing. I slowly enter the pool and clear my throat.

"Okay," I say, crossing my arms across my chest, not that there's much to cover in the first place.

Ethan turns around and asks, "Are you sure you're okay? You seem scared like you don't know me." Ethan places his hand on the side of my arm.

"I am nervous," I admit. "I've never done this before. No one's ever wanted to do this with me."

Ethan smooths his hair, slicking it back with his wet hand. "You mean, no one's been lucky enough to do this with you?"

A small smile manages to make its way onto my face. "I guess not," I reply, still slightly uncomfortable.

Ethan puts his other hand on my opposite arm, staying at arms-length.

"We can just enjoy the sunset," he suggests gently.

I look up at Ethan. I'm sure he's been with a lot of women since high school. I don't even need to ask him to know his answer.

"I, um. I don't want to *just* enjoy the sunset," I reply.

Ethan pulls my unclothed body closer to his and places his delicious lips on mine. I remove my arms that are tightly wrapped around my chest, no longer hiding my vulnerability. Ethan's hands move down my arms, graze my rear, and find their place on the back of my thighs. Ethan presses himself firmly against my body as he guides my thighs upward and forward, urging me to spread my legs and sit on his lap. Once I am seated to his liking, Ethan pushes my back against the side of the pool wall and kisses me like he's never kissed me before.

Ethan whispers into my ear, "I want you back."

"I thought that was pretty clear when you sent me the plane ticket," I reply.

I place both my arms along the edge of the pool and let Ethan transport me to another planet. After all, he is more experienced than I am.

The sun has fallen. I look up at the full moon and thousands of stars twinkling in the darkened sky.

"So, Zoe, will you take me back?" Ethan asks in a sultry voice.

My eyes involuntarily close and roll to the back of my head. I am unable to respond. Euphoria sparks throughout my body like stars exploding—pleasures I've never experienced, and now I can officially say… I am Ethan's girl.

Story Two

I Want You Now

Chapter One

Best Gift

Losing myself didn't seem so bad. I liked the new me. The new me was no longer mediocre, boring, or a virgin. I finally had a boyfriend and saw no tinge of loneliness in my future. Lee has come to terms with my new look and has given up on trying to get me to revert to my "old ways."

I lean against the side of my car, waiting for Ethan to walk out of the airport. It had been a long couple of months waiting for Ethan to come home for the holidays, and the anticipation was gnawing at my insides just thinking about our night in the pool when I visited him up North.

I wrap my pea-coat around my body, and then I notice Ethan. He drops his luggage on the sidewalk, anxiously picks me up, and spins me around.

"Ah, I've missed you, gorgeous," Ethan says.

I have a permanent grin on my face. "Ditto," I reply.

As we drive to my studio, Ethan mentions, "So, my family is having their big Christmas party in the evening tomorrow."

"On Christmas day?" I ask, worried. Ethan looks over at me like I asked a dumb question. I try to clarify and explain, "Well, I guess I should have mentioned I always spend Christmas day with Lee and his family."

"Like I said, the party is in the evening, so you should be fine. I thought you were going to say you needed to see Trish and her family. Well, anyway, you can do what you need to do during the day and meet me at my parents' house at night." Ethan places his hand on top of my thigh and gives it a couple of pats. "You wouldn't want to miss out on the gift I got you."

When I said "day," I meant the *whole* day, including the evening. Lee is going to kill me if I decide to bail early.

"I see Trish the morning after Christmas," I explain.

Ethan looks at me, confused. "Why do you see her the day after?"

"I know it's weird," I reply. "But she's so preoccupied on Christmas Eve and the day of. You know, with the kids and cooking all day. I can't really spend time with her while she's busy. We always go out to get these Christmas doughnuts down the street from her place. They are half-off the day after."

"All right…" Ethan says like he didn't really want to hear about my holiday routine, but I guess I should be flattered he wants me all to himself.

"Um, so, what does your family usually do for Christmas?" I ask.

"Kind of the typical family dinner, but a potluck."

"Does that mean I should bring something?"

"That would probably be a good idea. If you could make a dish, I'm sure my family would appreciate it."

Holy cow. Why did I even ask? You are aware I don't know how to cook, but Ethan isn't, and neither is his family.

I grip the steering wheel a little tighter before asking my next question. "So, how docs your family feel about macaroni and cheese from a box?"

Ethan looks at me, confused. "Oh," he laughs. "You're joking."

I roll with it. "Yeah… just… joking," I say quietly and fake chuckle to myself.

"I can ask my mom what she thinks and let you know," Ethan replies. "It will be easier, so you don't have to guess what kind of dish is needed."

My insides are churning, thinking of what kind of food I will have to cook, or more like, destroy.

We are about five minutes away from my studio. "I just want to warn you that my place is pretty small," I tell Ethan.

"Thanks for the warning," Ethan says, but now I think Ethan will be regretting staying with me while he's in town.

I unlock the door to my studio. "Ta-da," I say while holding out my arms.

Ethan walks inside, sets down his suitcases, and looks around. "Not bad, very homey," he mentions.

"I know. It's not much, but rent is ridiculous in San Diego, and I don't make a ton walking dogs and babysitting," I say, trying to give an explanation.

Ethan nods his head, pulls off his coat, and tosses it on the couch. "I think my favorite part is your bed."

He walks over to the edge of my mattress and takes a seat. Ethan smirks and pats the space beside him, ordering me to sit next to him.

"You look even more attractive than last time I saw you," he says.

I remove my coat too and toss it on top of his. I walk toward Ethan, but instead of sitting next to him, I take a seat on his lap, once again.

Oh, so anyway, this is the story of how I ended up losing my best friend.

Chapter Two

Fake It Until You Make It

I've been at Lee's all Christmas morning. I glance at the time, knowing I should leave soon to give myself enough time to make the potato salad Ethan's mom had instructed me to bring.

"You should open your present now," I tell Lee and hand him his gift.

"What? Really?" Lee asks, surprised. "You aren't going to make me wait until after dinner like you always do?"

Lee takes the box from my hand, and I begin to explain, "Yeah, um, so about that… You know how Ethan is in town?"

I nervously tug at the ugly sweater I've worn on Christmas the last ten years. It's custom at Lee's. Everyone has to wear the most ridiculous sweater, which is much better than getting all dressed up.

"Of course, I do. You've only talked about it nonstop the last one-hundred days."

"I have to leave soon," I murmur.

"Huh? Did you just say you have to leave early?"

I nod and cringe. Lee looks pissed.

Lee throws his hands up in annoyance. "Zoe, you've bailed on fro-yo a bunch of times, and now you're ditching out on Christmas dinner?" Lee repeatedly shakes his head. "Whatever, Zoe. Do whatever you want," he says, angrily.

"I'm sorry. I know I've been a terrible friend lately. If you would just open your present, maybe you will forgive me." I grin widely—hopeful.

Lee looks down at the unwrapped gift and sighs. Lee looks more than just disappointed and unwraps his present.

I giggle as Lee tries to suppress a smile. "You love it, don't you?" I ask.

He stares at the picture frame that holds a memory of one of our first times getting fro-yo together. We are seated at an outside table. Lee has his arm draped across my back. My hair is in its classic frizzy side braid, and Lee didn't have all his muscles yet.

Lee nods. "Yeah, I love it." He nudges the side of my arm with his.

"So, does that mean you forgive me?" I clasp my hands together under my chin and give him my best puppy dog eyes.

"Yeah. I guess." Lee gives me a side hug.

"Okay, where's my present?" I ask. I close my eyes and hold out my hands.

It feels like a piece of paper that Lee has placed onto my palms. I open my eyes to find a red envelope.

"Aw, money? You shouldn't have," I say sarcastically.

"Why would I give you money? I already pay for all our fro-yo dates and give you free training sessions at the gym."

I roll my eyes and tear open the envelope. The card is homemade. Lee has printed out a picture of Edward Cullen's shiny, vampire face.

"Your photoshop skills are excellent," I joke.

"You don't like the Santa hat I gave him?" Lee asks. "That took me a straight hour."

"It's pretty awesome," I reply.

"Just wait until you read what's inside," Lee says. He tilts his head up like he's high and mighty, grins, and proudly crosses his arms across his chest.

I look at him like he's gone mad. "Okay…"

The card reads:

Merry Christmas Zoe,

We have been friends since the first grade,
And you know for a fact that,
I've always been fond of your side braid.

You have made me watch Twilight,
About a million times too many,
But any time spent with you is a true highlight.

Even though fro-yo seems to be overdue,
I still can't wait for those dates,
Because there's no one else like you.

Love, Lee

I cover my mouth and chuckle. "All right. I should start calling you Jay-Z instead of Lee. You never told me you can write rhymes!" I shove Lee's shoulder. "You could make big bucks coming up with raps for artists," I joke.

"Shut up, Zoe," Lee says and glares at me. "If you're just going to crack jokes about the poem, I'll take it back." Lee reaches for the card.

I yank it away from him. "No, no! I'm just kidding. I love the poem," I say, and hold it to my heart for a moment, but then I realize I have stayed past the time I intended to. "Hey, Lee. I really am sorry, but I have to go." I quickly gather my belongings and shove the card to the bottom of my purse.

Lee looks bummed and doesn't say another word.

"Yogurt, next week!" I yell and point to Lee as I head toward the door. "I promise!"

When I get back to my studio, I turn on a how-to-video on my phone.

"Oh, I have to wash the potatoes?" I ask the lady who's in the video. I rip open the bag and toss them into the sink.

She tells me they need a good scrub to get all the dirt off, and then she starts peeling the spuds.

I scramble to find my peeler, searching through four different drawers before finding it. Holy cow, she's good at peeling those potatoes. I might lose a couple of layers of skin doing this. It's dangerous work, and it doesn't help I keep looking at the time, which is ticking by faster and faster.

Luckily, Ethan had gone over to his parents to help set up everything and spend time with the family. How embarrassing would this have been if I had an audience? I can't even manage to make potato salad.

"I can do this!" I scream aloud to myself and try to peel a little faster. "There's, like, fifty potatoes!"

I throw the peeled spuds into the boiling water, but by now, I should have just arrived at the party.

"Come on, cook faster!" I yell at the pot of boiling water. I haven't even cut up any of the other ingredients. "Shit!" I say and angrily turn off the burner.

I realize Ethan has just text me: "*Are you on your way?*"

I discard the evidence of my failed, partially made dish, grab a glass bowl along with my keys, and head to the grocery store. I mean, no one will ever know the difference between homemade and grocery store potato salad, right? I didn't want Ethan to think I was an incompetent cook. Remember, I told you, guys like a girl who can take care of them like my sister. Dang, too bad Trish is swamped cooking a ten-course Christmas meal for her family, or she could've made the potato salad for me. Oh well.

I text Ethan I'm standing outside his parents' house. Ethan opens the door and stares at me, surprised. For a second, I think Ethan's looking at the bowl of potato salad I'm holding in my hands, but then I realize he's looking at my ugly sweater. Oops. I forgot to change, and I also forgot to mention my "ugly sweater" is an *inappropriate* ugly sweater. It reads, "Santa's Twerk Shop," and it has Santa… well, obviously doing his thing, twerking. Lee's family thought it was funny the first time I wore it, and it was only $1.89 at the thrift store—such a steal.

I met Ethan's family a few times when we were dating. I don't know why Ethan told me this, but he mentioned his parents thought I was a bad influence on him. I look down at my sweater again. Hmm… I wonder why they would possibly think that. Great. Well, anyway, they were always so hospitable and nice to me. I would've never guessed in a hundred years that Ethan's parents felt that way about me. I guess his parents were pros at faking it.

"Here, let me take that," Ethan says, grabbing the bowl out of my hands. I try to follow him to the table, but Ethan's mom hurriedly walks up to me.

Grace grabs my hand and holds it in hers. "Zoe, there you are. I didn't recognize you with your new hairdo. You look more lovely than ever, and Ethan told me you guys got back together. I can't tell you how happy that makes me."

Ethan's mom should've picked up a career as an actress. "Yup," I reply uncomfortably.

Grace looks at my outfit and lets go of my hand. She takes a step back to get a better view of my sweater. "Oh, uh, Santa's... That's an interesting choice for a sweater."

She continues to stare with the most disgusted look on her face. Grace tries to hide her expression behind her hand, but it's a little too late for that. Too bad I'm not wearing anything underneath, or I would've taken my sweater off by now. I bet I'm the only person on the planet not smart enough to wear anything under her ugly sweater on Christmas.

Ethan's mom clears her throat, regains her composure, points at me, and asks, "So, where did you get that *darling* sweater?"

Phil, Ethan's dad, joins us. I look over my shoulder and see that Ethan has gotten tied up talking to one of his relatives.

"Nice, Santa's Twerk Shop, huh?" Phil says. "You steal that off a bum?" he jokes.

"Mhmm," I reply as I try to play along, but inside I'm dying from embarrassment. "That's exactly where I got it from."

"You were always such a jokester," Phil adds. I can smell the boozy eggnog radiating from his breath.

Finally, Ethan makes his way over to his parents and me. "Zoe made the potato salad you asked her to make," he mentions.

"Oh, that's wonderful, Zoe," his mom tells me and places her hand on my shoulder. Grace quickly retracts her hand, probably appalled by my sweater. I bet she thinks she's going to catch leprosy from it.

"I can't wait to give it a try," Phil chimes in.

Me either, I think to myself. "It's not anything special," I reply, trying to lower their expectations. "It probably doesn't taste any better than the… store-bought kind."

"You are so modest," Grace says while laughing.

"If you don't mind, I'm going to steal Zoe now since I haven't seen her all day. I still have to give Zoe her present," Ethan tells his parents and holds my hand to pull me somewhere more private, and I am beyond grateful.

As Ethan takes me outside to his backyard, I know I look disappointed. "I forgot to change before I came over. Ugly sweaters are a tradition at Lee's." I keep trying to justify my outfit, "I usually wouldn't—"

"Shh. It's fine. Really," Ethan says, trying to reassure me, and holds me tightly underneath a large willow tree. I don't remember it being so big the last time I was over.

I feel my phone vibrate in my pocket. "Sorry," I tell Ethan as I pull away from his embrace. "Someone texted me," I explain.

And that someone was Lee. He texted me: "*Grandma Betty won Holiday Mahjong again. Can you believe it? My mom's so mad. She's trying to hide her anger by cooking another round of food. Everyone's asking where you are and wanted me to tell you Merry Christmas.*"

I smile as I finish reading Lee's text, but my heart also feels heavy, remembering how much I love spending time with his family—my family.

"What's going on. Is everything okay?" Ethan asks.

"Nothing, everything's great," I reply and fake a smile. I wrap my arms around Ethan and lay my head on his chest. "Where were we?"

"I want to ask you something," he replies. "I thought this was the best Christmas present I could offer you."

"Hmm. What's that?" I ask, continuing to think about how I bailed on Lee and his family.

"Would you ever consider moving to Northern California?"

I laugh. "What? Why would I do that?" I ask, confused and still distracted by my guilty thoughts of missing Christmas dinner with Lee.

"Zoe," Ethan says and pulls away slightly to look into my eyes. "So, we can be closer."

"Oh, sorry. I didn't realize what you were asking."

"Are you sure everything is fine?"

I nod my head. "I would love to be closer to you, but my job and… everything is here."

Ethan looks more irritated than sad. He's probably not used to girls saying no to him.

"Well, I have three more weeks to convince you," he says, and Ethan's demeanor changes to swoony. "It's a nice night out."

"Yeah," I agree.

Ethan looks up and then back at me. "What?" I ask.

"Look up," Ethan says.

I tilt my head back and notice mistletoe strung on a branch of the willow tree. I chuckle. "I didn't notice that hanging there." I abruptly stop giggling once I realize Ethan's gaze is fixated, hard on my eyes.

"Zoe, I need to tell you that being with you is one of the best Christmas presents you could've given me." Ethan pulls me in closer. "Every time I'm with you, I don't want to let you go. I don't ever want to let you go. I can't help it. I feel like you are a magnet drawing me in, and I can't seem to pull away."

Ethan leaves me speechless. I swallow the lump in my throat. Ethan places his hand behind the back of my head and kisses me. I don't understand how his kisses get better each time. Every kiss that follows sends me into the never-ending abyss of what I think might be love.

Chapter Three

Doughnut Hole

The next morning, Trish and I spend some time together at our usual doughnut shop.

"Thank goodness, they didn't sell out of the old-fashioned ones," Trish says, referring to the glazed doughnuts covered with holiday sprinkles.

"I don't know how you can eat those," I mention. "There's more sugar than doughnut."

The lady behind the counter hands Trish two of the most sugary doughnuts in the world. Talk about a sugar overload.

"Can I just get a half-dozen of the doughnut holes, please?" I ask the lady while pointing to the red and green balls.

"Once you have kids of your own, you won't judge my love for a sugar rush," Trish explains as we take a seat at a table. "Also, I'm eating for two." Trish grins and holds up her doughnut like she's giving a toast. "Cheers," she says and takes a bite.

"Rough Christmas?" I ask.

"Always, but worth it," she replies. "How was yours?"

"It was good."

"Just good? Didn't beat Grandma Betty at Mahjong this year?"

"I went to Ethan's family's party last night."

"And?" Trish asks and then takes another bite, almost finishing the entire doughnut.

"And… Ethan wants me to move up North."

Trish's eyes widen, taken aback. "Oh, my gosh. Seriously?"

"I know, so crazy, right?" I reply.

"I mean… It is a little. Kind of spur of the moment is all, but hmm…" Trish ponders for a minute.

"What?" I ask impatiently, wanting to know her thoughts.

"Well, I'm curious. What does Lee think about it?"

"I haven't told Lee yet."

"I bet he'd be pretty disappointed if his best friend moved hours away from him, don't you think?"

"Probably, but it's not like I'm going to do it anyway."

"You sure about that?" Trish asks. "You seemed pretty infatuated with Ethan the last few months. Plus, you are kind of obsessing with how you look. I'm surprised you even agreed to eat doughnuts with me today."

I glare at Trish, annoyed. "I still eat normal foods. I eat burgers religiously, and I wouldn't go as far to say… infatuated."

"Okay, Zoe. If you say so. Maybe I should say Ethan is more infatuated with you. If I remember correctly, you were telling me how Ethan invited you out to see him and got you into the pool within two minutes of walking into your hotel room."

I roll my eyes. "It wasn't two minutes after we walked into the room."

Trish looks at me sternly—the same way she looks at her kids after they tell a fib.

"Fine!" I shout. "It was more like five minutes, okay?"

She slowly nods her head repeatedly like she knows every single detail of my relationship with Ethan. "And I bet I can guess what you guys did right when Ethan got into town the other day."

I cross my arms, wanting to keep those specifics to myself so Trish can't place more judgment on me. I confidently say, "I have absolutely no idea what you are referring to."

Trish slams her palms down on the table, and her face scrunches up in frustration. "Oh, please, Zoe!" She points her finger at my face. "You know what you did."

I stick my nose up toward the ceiling, denying Trish's assumptions. "I don't have the slightest clue what you're talking about."

"This is what you did," Trish says and picks up her second doughnut. She holds the sugary treat in the air, and using her other hand, she repeatedly sticks her index finger through the middle where the hole is in the doughnut.

"Holy cow, Trish!" I shout. "People are staring!"

She nonchalantly takes a bite out of the doughnut. "Well, that's what you get for trying to play dumb with me."

"I wasn't trying to play—"

"Just don't, Zoe. I know you did the *nasty* as soon as Ethan stepped off that plane."

I lean forward toward Trish. "Oh, my gosh, Trish, why do you have to say that? You always make things so awkward."

"Don't you dare change the subject, Zoe."

"Fine! We did! We did the *nasty*. Are you happy now?" I whisper angrily.

Trish nods her head. "Yeah, glad you can finally say it out loud."

"Well, I don't see what's wrong with being attracted to someone," I fume.

"Calm down. I'm not trying to be a mean sister. All I'm trying to say is that it takes more than physical attraction to keep a relationship going. There's nothing wrong with being attracted to someone, but I just find it kind of strange your appearance drastically changed overnight, and suddenly, Ethan's all about it."

"I feel like you're saying Ethan isn't interested in my personality."

"Don't start twisting my words around. That's not at all what I said."

"I'm pretty sure that's what I heard," I say defensively.

Trish sighs in frustration and tries to explain herself. "I'm just saying that it's a little ironic, is all. Didn't you say Ethan told you he didn't love you when he broke up with you in high school, and didn't he end up getting with some other girl?"

I didn't expect to have this conversation with my sister, especially on our "day after Christmas" hangout.

"Trish, I really don't want to talk about this. You should remember," I say. "I'm your big sister. Not the other way around. So, you shouldn't be giving me advice on relationships."

"Don't go there," Trish says, annoyed. "I'm just trying to be helpful. It all seems kind of rushed. You run into Ethan again one day, and then the next he's asking you to move hundreds of miles away from us, but if you feel like moving closer to Ethan is the right thing to do, then do it. No one's stopping you. Just remember, the honeymoon stage is a total of two years, and after that stage is over, and you have kids, there's the roommate stage."

"Yes, Trish. I'm aware of all the 'stages' you claim to be an actual thing," I reply in a snooty tone.

"Take it from me, Zoe. They are very real, and I've experienced both with Roy."

"Can't you just be happy that I'm happy?" I ask. "Ethan finally wants to be with me."

I think I've made Trish feel bad by mentioning my happiness because now she looks more sympathetic rather than frustrated.

She reaches across the table, grabs my hand, and gives it a good squeeze before replying, "Oh, Zoe. Yes, that's all I ever want for you. So, yeah. If you're happy, then I'm happy, but if things don't work out according to plan, the last thing I want is to see you upset. There are a lot of other potential guys out there."

I have a hard time believing Trish. I guess I still haven't gotten over the whole low self-esteem issue. Even though I might look like a different person on the outside, I still feel like the same old boring Zoe on the inside—kind of like one of those spruced-up doughnuts with fancy sprinkles with a hole in the middle. Not sure why Lee thinks I've been acting any different. I think he's got it all wrong, and so does my sister.

Chapter Four

Fro-yo or Fro-no

"It feels like a lifetime since we've gotten some fro-yo," Lee says as we stand in line, which always seems to be wrapped around the building.

"I know, but at least we're here now," I mention. "You should let me treat you today to make up for when I had to ditch the last couple of times."

"Wow, Zoe's offering to treat?" Lee asks sarcastically. "I thought this day would never come."

"Shut up," I say and slap the side of his shoulder. "You are the worst."

"Am I, though? I didn't leave my family's Christmas party to go hang out with a guy, and I'm pretty sure I haven't been skipping out on fro-yo or taking advantage of your job."

I roll my eyes. "Fine! *I'm* the worst," I admit. "I'm a terrible friend."

Luckily, Ethan had some work e-mails he needed to attend to today, so I was able to make some time to hang out with Lee.

Lee bringing up Christmas makes me think about what Ethan had mentioned when we were standing underneath the willow tree. I knew eventually I would have to tell Lee. Maybe now would be a good time. I am curious to find out what he thinks if I were to ever leave. I might as well just bring it up now. Now is as good of a time as ever, I suppose.

"So, that actually reminds me," I say. "On Christmas—"

"Hey, Bruce!" a voice in front of us interrupts me.

I see some girl a few people ahead of us is waving excitedly at Lee.

"You know her?" I ask.

"Looks like one of the girls I've had a couple of training sessions with this last month."

The petite girl tells one of her girlfriends she will be right back and walks over to us like a dog excitedly greeting its master. I don't think I've ever seen anyone with as silky hair as hers—super light brown, which could be confused as blonde.

"Hi, Cynthia," Lee says.

Cynthia doesn't acknowledge my presence and continues to talk to Lee. I think I should probably get used to these kinds of encounters since we had that run-in with Margo at the reunion, and now this.

"Maybe I should've acted like I didn't see you. I know how you feel about your *trainees* cheating and eating unhealthy," Cynthia giggles and grins at Lee, twisting her body side to side with her hands clasped together in front of her.

"Well, I can't say much now since you caught me standing in line too," Lee replies.

I continue to stay silent, admiring Cynthia's perfect ivory skin, which looks like it's never been touched by a single sunray, and Cynthia's flirtatious vibes are kind of overwhelming to watch. Now, she's playfully touching the hem of her skirt. The only time I've ever seen someone wearing a hoochie schoolgirl outfit was on a Britney Spears' music video. Well, good for Cynthia, seeing as I wouldn't be able to pull off an outfit like that.

"Do you want to join me and my friend?" Cynthia asks Lee, pointing to a table, which is not one of the usual tables Lee and I sit at.

Lee looks at me for an answer. "Uh, I don't know. Do you want to?"

"Oh," Cynthia says. She looks at me, leans slightly forward, and places her hand gently on her chest. "How rude of me... You are?"

Did I mention Cynthia looks like one of those girls from a K-pop group? Yeah, she's really got it goin' on, to say the least.

"Zoe," I answer, forcing a smile.

"So, *Zoe*, what do you say? Would you like to join Emma and me for some yogurt?" Cynthia asks.

"Mhmm," I reply and look at Lee as I accidentally begin talking an octave too high. "That sounds… fantastic."

It really doesn't sound fantastic. It's always just Lee and me when we enjoy our yogurts, and she picked the wrong table. I wish Lee would've turned Cynthia down instead of putting the blame on me, making me look like the antisocial one, if I refused her offer. I'm pretty sure Cynthia doesn't want my company anyway.

After purchasing our yogurts, we join the two girls.

"This is the amazing trainer I've been telling you about," Cynthia mentions to Emma, who looks like she's a part of Cynthia's K-pop group.

Cynthia gently touches the side of Lee's arm and smiles. She turns toward her friend, and they both giggle.

"I'm only as amazing as my clients are," Lee replies, ignoring Cynthia's blunt body language. "If they aren't willing to put in the effort and work, then I can't promise results."

Cynthia stays persistent and turns her body toward Lee. "It's so hard to get to know you at the gym. I'm always out of breath and panting like a poor dog. Your workouts are so intense," she says and crosses her legs toward Lee. She even touches his arm a second time. "But you know I like it."

Cynthia looks like she wants nothing more than to mount Lee's lap. I feel like I should be closing my eyes like a little kid witnessing a dirty scene on TV for the very first time. I attempt to focus on eating my yogurt.

"I try to do my job to the best of my abilities," Lee responds and continues to enjoy his fro-yo. Lee doesn't really seem all that fazed by Cynthia throwing herself at him.

"So, Bruce. Tell us more about yourself. What are you into?" Cynthia asks enthusiastically.

"I'm a pretty boring guy. Not too much to brag about," Lee says.

"Well, you're in luck. *I'm* not boring at all," Cynthia says. "I can keep you entertained for hours."

Okay, so that could mean something inappropriate, or my mind might just be in the gutter. Either way, I feel like I'm sitting in on Lee's and Cynthia's first date.

"That's chill," Lee replies. He abruptly stands up. I guess Lee has finished his yogurt. I quickly take another bite, stick my spoon in my cup, and stand up too. "Okay, ladies, I'll catch you later," he adds.

"Oh, um, all right," Cynthia says, disappointed. "I guess I will see you next week at the gym."

Cynthia tries to get Lee's attention and stands up too. I think she was going for a hug, but Lee had already turned his back to her.

"Bye, Cynthia, Emma… nice to meet you," I say awkwardly and wave. Emma waves back, but Cynthia continues to stand in place and glare at me. "Okay, um, bye… again," I murmur and turn quickly to catch up with Lee.

We hop into my car. "What was that all about?" I ask.

Lee shrugs.

"Cynthia is smokin' hot," I say.

Lee shrugs again.

"That chick wanted you, like, *really* wanted you, bad," I say and start the ignition. "She would've ripped off her panties in the fro-yo shop if you asked her to."

I look over at Lee, but he is silent, gazing out the window.

"You look upset," I mention and turn the ignition off. "She might be worth pursuing," I say.

I mean, she might warm up to me. Cynthia probably thought Lee and I were seeing each other like Margo assumed at the reunion.

Lee shakes his head. "Not my type," he says flatly.

"Are you kidding me?" I ask, shocked. "She's perfect. Cynthia looks like she could be some famous pop artist in Korea, and I bet she can make some banging bulgogi. You know, that one delicious, marinaded meat we had at the BBQ restaurant your parents took me to for my twentieth birthday. Holy cow. That was the best—"

"I told you she's not my type," Lee says through a clenched jaw.

"I don't understand. No one's been your type for the last decade. Now you have all these girls throwing themselves at you, and you can't give one of them a chance?"

Lee shakes his head, annoyed. "You just don't get it, Zoe."

"Well, can you explain it to me? I want to understand. I just don't get it. I mean, no one wants to be alone."

"Can we just drop this subject?" Lee asks.

"I guess. If you promise you aren't mad at me."

"I'm not mad, Zoe." Lee sighs. "Why don't you finish telling me what you wanted to earlier."

"Hmm?"

"When we were waiting in line, you wanted to tell me something."

Well, if Lee isn't mad at me now, I have a strong feeling he will be in a minute, especially after I tell him what happened on Christmas, or maybe Lee won't mind at all. Who am I kidding? Talk about wishful thinking. Here goes nothing.

"Ethan mentioned I should move to Northern California with him." I cringe, waiting for Lee's response.

"That's insane," Lee says calmly in a monotone voice.

"Is it?" I ask. "I mean, yeah. It is, huh?"

Then out of nowhere, I see fire in Lee's eyes. "Oh, my gosh. You are considering it, aren't you?"

"I—I, um—" I murmur.

"I can't believe it! You would have to be out of your mind to just up and leave all you know behind." Lee squishes his head between his hands. "That's not fair to you. Why doesn't *Ethan* move to San Diego for *you*? If you mean that much to him, he would make that happen."

"Well… for one thing, I don't own a multimillion-dollar company."

"That's the dumbest thing I've ever heard," Lee replies.

I'm pretty sure the anger is influencing Lee's words. Trish was right—Lee doesn't want to lose his best friend.

"It's not like I told him I would move."

"Good. Because—because that would just be so stupid. You barely know the guy," Lee says sharply.

Would it be stupid? I don't know. It could be a good thing, and what is Lee talking about? I *know* Ethan. Okay, not as well as Lee or my sister, but it's different. I don't have the same relationship with Trish or my best friend. With Ethan… it's different.

"Don't do it, Zoe," Lee adds.

I know how to get Lee to stop fuming. "I won't. My home is here," I say, and it works. I notice Lee's breathing slow, and his face doesn't look as tense.

I finally start the car up again. "Want to go to my place and watch *Breaking Dawn*?" I ask.

Lee can't help but reveal a little smile.

"I know you want to," I say, poking Lee on the side of his arm before pulling out of the parking spot.

"But isn't Ethan at your studio?" Lee asks.

"No, he likes to sort through his work e-mails at the park," I reply.

"Oh, cool." Lee looks at me and smirks. "*Twilight* it is then." Lee punches his arm out in front of him and shouts, "Team Jacob, for life!"

Chapter Five

Convince Me

Right after the movie ended, Lee mentions something about intruding on Ethan's and my "alone" time.

"You should stay for dinner," I tell him. "I'm sure Ethan would love hanging out with you too."

"What are you guys having?" Lee asks.

"I'm making spaghetti."

Lee points at me, surprised. "*You* are making spaghetti?" Then, he busts up laughing.

I shoot Lee a dirty look. "Yeah… how difficult can it be? It's kind of like making mac and cheese from a box. I just have to add some ground beef, and instead of cheese sauce, I will use a can of tomato sauce," I explain defensively.

"Don't get all worked up. So, tell me, when did you pick up cooking?" Lee asks.

"Since… about a week ago," I say. It sounded more like a question than a statement when it came out of my mouth. "So, does that mean you will stay for dinner?"

"I think I'm going to pass. Don't want to risk getting E. coli."

I give Lee the most sinister glare I can conjure. "Fine, just leave," I say, annoyed, and turn my back to him.

Lee gives me a big bear hug. "I'm only messing around. Maybe one of these days, I will take one for the team and try out your cooking, but hopefully, it's just a phase, and it won't come to that."

I try to wriggle out of Lee's hold. "Shut it!" I shout, trying to pull Lee's larger-than-life arms from my body. "Let me go. You're such a bully."

"Never!" Lee yells, but he lets go and starts tickling my ribs.

"What are we… five again?" I scream through my laughter.

Lee doesn't let up. I try to evade him, but Lee's attacks have caused me to stumble and fall flat on my back onto the floor. Somehow, when I crash-landed, my legs became entangled between Lee's, which made him lose his balance too, causing him to fall on top of me.

"Ow!" I shout. "I think you crushed my spleen," I wince.

"Oh, don't be such a baby," Lee says and pushes himself up into a pushup position.

Lee continues to hover over my body, staring at me. "Um," I chuckle, expecting him to have picked himself up by now. "What are you doing?"

Lee looks confused for a moment and possibly in a daze.

"Earth to Lee," I say and wave my hand in front of his face.

His eyes finally look a little less glazed over, and Lee replies, "Zoe, I need to tell you something."

"Okay, what is it?" I ask.

Lee looks directly into my eyes like he is about to tell me something that will impact whether we live or die—something so serious, it could send the planet off its axis. "I want to tell you before it's too late, and I know you are seeing—"

Nearby, someone clears his throat loudly. Lee and I both abruptly turn our heads toward the door.

"Should I come back another time?" Ethan asks sharply.

I shake my head in a panic and push Lee with all my might, causing Lee to clumsily roll off me. Or maybe Lee voluntarily removed himself. Probably the second assumption. Doesn't matter though, because, either way, I can only imagine what's going through Ethan's mind. Maybe it was a bad idea to give Ethan my spare key while he's visiting.

"No, no. There's nothing going on," I reply nervously, sitting up and straightening out my shirt.

Lee sits on the floor for a minute and says something about him overstaying his welcome. Ethan is silent and continues to stand in the same spot by the door, clenching his jaw tightly.

"You don't have to leave, Lee," I say, but Lee hurriedly heads toward the exit, brushing his shoulder against Ethan's, and doesn't say another word before rushing out the door.

Ethan tosses his jacket on the couch, and I can tell there's rage building inside of him. Ethan takes a seat, folds his hands on his lap, and looks at me through the corner of his eye.

"Do you want to explain yourself?" he asks.

"Um, well, we were just watching a movie, and Lee was just about to leave," I reply anxiously. "I tripped and… Lee… fell on top of me."

Ethan leans back onto the couch and looks at me like I murdered someone. "He fell on top of you? Did his mouth accidentally land on yours too in the process?"

"Ew!" I shout, trying to make the best exaggerated "yucky" face I can. "We would never, ever, *ever* do—"

I hurriedly run around the couch to take a seat by Ethan to look him directly in his eyes and show him the expression on my face that I'm currently trying to hold in place. I set my hand on top of Ethan's, hoping he will open his closed hands for me to caress, but as I do this, I accidentally picture kissing Lee… but only because Ethan brought it up!

"I know that sounds like a lie, but it's not," I continue, trying to defend the truth. "Lee and I have been friends since elementary school. That would just be weird!" I chuckle uncomfortably.

Ethan rubs the bottom of his chin like he's deciding whether he believes me or not. Thankfully, he leaves one of his hands under mine, so there's still hope he will forgive me.

"I promise, Lee and I are only friends. Nothing more," I assure Ethan.

Ethan flips his hand over and gives my hand a firm squeeze. "All right," he says. "I believe you."

I place my other hand on my chest. "Phew!" I say. "You had me worried for a minute."

Ethan gives me a slanted smile. "So, have you given it any more thought—about moving in with me?"

I look at Ethan, confused. "Moving in with you?"

"Yeah."

"But on Christmas, didn't you say move *closer* to you? Not *in*… with you."

"You are correct, but I was thinking it would be beneficial for both of us if you just moved into my house with me."

"How so?" I ask, trying not to act too surprised.

"Your studio is so small, and you mentioned rent is expensive. If you moved in with me, you wouldn't have to pay rent. Prices aren't drastically different where I live, but I would be more than happy to take care of you."

I chuckle, thinking Ethan is crazy. "I couldn't mooch off you. I would feel like a freeloader."

"I know you would do your part. It wouldn't be freeloading. I could use a homecooked meal when I get home from work. Usually, my brain is overloaded by the time I return home, and I throw a TV dinner in the microwave and call it dinner. I should probably eat less processed foods if I'm to live past sixty."

"I don't know, Ethan. Everything I know is here in San Diego."

"What's in San Diego that's more important than starting a life with me? If you are worried about moving in and it not working out between us, you don't need to fret about that. I want to settle down. I will be just as invested in our relationship as you are. I got so caught up in my work and just messing around, dating women who want to play games. I've come to realize it's time for me to find someone who wants to play for keeps, and you are exactly what I've been looking for."

That was a good speech Ethan just gave—somewhat convincing. What's keeping me in San Diego? Answer: Trish, Ashley, Travis… and *Lee*… of course, but I don't dare say that out loud.

"Please, move in with me," Ethan continues. He straightens up and turns his body toward mine, caressing my hand in both of his. Ethan looks me in the eyes like a desperate man. "You have me begging you already. I don't know what else I can do to convince you. I promise you won't regret living with me."

I start to imagine myself in a white gown, walking down a long church aisle. Ethan looks handsome in his tux as he awaits to take my hand in marriage. Our wedding night ends with him ripping off my wedding dress and ravaging my body, which is completely fine now that we are married. Trish wouldn't be able to place judgment on me anymore. Okay, and fast forward a year later—my belly is round with a baby girl. I'm happily preparing dinner for Ethan before he comes home. The meal I'm preparing smells like a dish on a cooking show prepared by a professional chef. Life is amazing. Wait. Rewind—who was walking me down the aisle at my wedding to give me away? No one. I am walking by myself, and I look frantic. I'm searching for comfort. Where is Lee? Is Lee in the audience? I don't see Lee at my imaginary wedding. He probably hates me and refused my invitation. I don't think I can live with Lee hating me, so I can't bring myself to agree to move in with Ethan.

"I will… strongly consider it," I reply.

Ethan smiles, "Okay, I will take that answer. At least it's not a no."

I excuse myself from the couch to make dinner. "Well, I better get cooking," I say. I'm glad I had an excuse to cut off the topic Ethan and I were on. "Cross your fingers and pray I don't burn the place down."

"You're quite the comedian," Ethan says.

Am I, though? I wasn't joking, but I guess I tried to hide the fact that I was actually serious. I still want Ethan to think I can make a meal.

"Yup, yup!" I reply.

That night, I lie in bed with Ethan. He is tuckered out from responding to his work e-mails, but more so from us doing the "nasty"—as Trish would say. Ethan's fast asleep, but I continue to toss and turn—my mind unable to turn itself off, thinking about the pros and cons of living with Ethan. Ethan makes me happy, and no one's ever put me on a pedestal like he has. I don't want to be alone my entire life. I think I can be that perfect girl for Ethan, and we can have a future together like he mentioned. Isn't that what every girl dreams of?

Chapter Six

Live Life

The next night, after the kids were put to bed, I drove over to talk to Trish. I sat on the kitchen barstool, hoping for an answer.

"You hate when I give you advice, but when I don't give you advice, you ask for my opinion anyway. You do realize this, right?" Trish says, grabbing a bottle of wine from one of the kitchen cabinets.

I roll my eyes. "Just tell me what you think I should do."

Trish drills the corkscrew into the top of the wine bottle and says, "I already told you what I think about you leaving."

"I know. I know. Just tell me again. Ethan was so convincing the other night. He gave me all these amazing reasons why I should move in with him, and now I can't help but think about *actually* doing it."

"Wait, let me get this straight. Now you aren't just thinking about moving closer to Ethan, you are going to live *with* him?"

"Um, yeah. You think it's a terrible idea, don't you?"

Trish shrugs and pours the wine into a glass and holds it up to her nose.

"What are you doing?" I ask.

She inhales deeply. "Here," she says, handing me the glass filled with wine.

"Uh, I still don't understand," I say.

Trish shoves the glass even closer toward my face. "Take it," she says. "Drink up. I want to live vicariously through you and pretend I'm the one downing this bottle."

I hesitantly take the glass from her hand. "Okay…"

"As soon as I get this baby out of me, I'm going to bathe in a tub filled with red wine."

"Please, don't," I reply.

"Don't judge," Trish says and points to the glass. "Drink."

I take a sip. This might be exactly what I need, to be honest.

Trish continues, "Listen, it kind of sounds like you've already made up your mind, but if you want my advice, not sugarcoated, do what makes you happy."

Trish forcefully grabs the glass out of my hand and takes a huge whiff before handing it back to me. I think she wants me to take another sip, so that's exactly what I do.

She goes on, "Live life and learn. Don't be afraid to take risks. Look where 'playing it safe' got me." She points to her husband passed out on the recliner with an empty beer bottle in his hand. "Don't get me wrong. I love him to death. I love my children, and I shouldn't complain about anything, but some days I feel like I didn't live life to the fullest getting married so young and popping those two little brats out so fast."

"Trish!" I shout.

"Remember when I told you I wanted to move to Los Angeles and become an actress?" she asks.

I nod and grin, thinking about how we bonded over her passion. "Yeah! Of course. I'm the one who stayed up endless nights, all night helping you run your lines over and over again for your acting classes and shows. How could I forget that?"

"Yeah, and you were always there, front row at all my performances." Trish smiles for a moment while she reminisces, but her happiness is soon wiped away as she returns to the subject of how her dream vanished. "Anyway, once I married Roy, my acting career seemed like a distant thought." I notice Trish's eyes seem glossy like she's trying to hold back tears. She shakes her head and looks down, saddened. "You probably think I'm so selfish for saying such a thing."

"Never, Sis," I say, reaching over the counter to grab her hand.

Trish looks up at me. "Truth is… although you probably think you should have what I have—a husband who supports his family and two kids that drive a mom crazy day in and day out—I'm the one who is envious of you."

"Oh, come on, Trish," I say. "That's ridiculous."

"It's true." Trish points her finger at me. "Find someone who truly loves you for who you are and not for what you can do to make *his* life better." She glances over at Roy for a second to make sure he's still asleep. "Find someone who will support you at anything you are doing or want to do in life."

"You are a good wife and mom," I tell Trish. "They are lucky to have you take such good care of them, and I don't blame you for wanting more credit for everything you do. You do so much for your family. I doubt they would be able to function more than a day without you."

I see a single tear trickle down my sister's cheek. "Ah," Trish stutters. She looks embarrassed, revealing this side of herself to me. "Look at me… being all dramatic. It must just be the pregnancy hormones talking." She wipes away the moisture on her face.

"Or maybe you can blame the wine that you're drinking," I joke, holding up the glass.

Trish chuckles softly.

"Hey, I *also* forgot to mention," I say, "how great of a sister you are."

Trish smiles at me. "You too," she says. "So, I guess my advice was kind of vague, huh?"

I nod my head. "Yeah." I laugh. "I still have no idea what I'm going to do."

But Trish was right about one thing—I had already made up my mind.

Chapter Seven

Bad News Second

I lie on my back on a mat at the gym as Lee takes me through some reps of leg lifts and other… what does he call them? Calisthenics? Yeah, something like that.

"I have some good news," Lee says.

I quickly stop exercising and prop myself up onto my elbow. "Did you finally get tickets to Comic-Con? I can guarantee the cast of *Twilight* won't be there."

Lee laughs and shakes his head. "No."

"Oh," I say sadly and lower myself back down to continue my pelvic thrusts.

"And I can assure you, if we ever do get tickets to Comic-Con, there are so many more important things we could do besides listening to actors and actresses talk about themselves."

My face scrunches up in confusion. What or who could possibly be more important? "Don't tell me, you would want to listen to a panel go on forever about Dungeons and Dragons?"

"You know you liked playing it with me."

I roll my eyes at Lee's incorrect assumption. "I hated that game, and if I remember correctly, I only played it with you because you were so obsessed with it in ninth grade. You wouldn't shut up about it, and I told you if we completed… what do you call it? Oh, yeah, 'the quest', you couldn't play for a week or talk about it."

Lee looks down and tries to act depressed. "And… that was the worst week of my life. How could you do that to me, Zoe?"

"Oh, please!" I yell.

Lee lifts his gaze—ending his theatrics and chuckles. "I can't believe I went a whole week without playing. You should let me give you some real training, and we can become professional Dungeon Masters."

"Now, why would I want to do that?" I ask, confused.

"People pay good money to join your game," Lee says enthusiastically. "I know a guy who makes a hundred dollars—AN HOUR." Lee clinches his fists. He looks like he's going to fall to his knees, becoming overwhelmed by his ridiculous fantasy.

That will never happen. "You're funny," I reply. Lee's thoughts are too farfetched.

"Oh, I'm dead serious, Zoe," Lee says.

I squint at Lee like he's lost it. "I'm going to have to suggest we don't quit our day jobs."

"It would be a side gig. Don't hate on the game."

I mean, I could use some extra money, but realistically, if I move in with Ethan, I wouldn't have to worry about that. I would be more concerned about cooking and taking care of him in that sense.

"What I really need training on is cooking. Your mom down for some culinary lessons?" I ask.

"Honestly, she would love spending time in the kitchen with you. You know how that's her thing," Lee responds. "How'd your pasta dinner turn out?"

"Not too bad," I reply. I think back to my potato salad disaster. "It could've been a lot worse."

"Darn. I was hoping you epically failed," Lee says.

I sit up and look at him questionably. I take a sip of my water before asking, "Why would you wish such a thing?"

Lee crosses his arms and looks around the gym like he's about to say something else that will push my buttons. "Oh, you know, so then I wouldn't have to worry about you going to live near Ethan."

Oh, great. I was hoping to postpone this subject—maybe like a week before I packed up my studio. Or, like, a couple of days before. I know, that's so terrible, but I didn't want to make Lee mad. At least I ended up making

Ethan really happy before he headed back to his place up North and gave him a solid answer.

"I'm so sad you have to leave," I told Ethan as he folded the remainder of his clothes and placed them neatly in his suitcase.

"Me too," Ethan said as he buckled the latches on his luggage.

Ethan turned toward me, and I gave him a sad puppy dog face. Ethan grabbed both of my hands.

"My offer still stands. We don't have to do this long-distance," Ethan said.

I smiled, excited to tell him my decision. "I want to take you up on your offer."

"What?" Ethan shouted, ecstatic. He released my hands and ran his hands through his hair like he won the lottery. "I can't believe it!"

"I know. I really kept you waiting, didn't I?"

Ethan picked me up by my waist and held me against him. I looked down into his dreamy eyes. "Man, I can't wait," he said. "You need to make this happen by the end of next month, or I will go crazy without you."

I heard his words and should've responded, but all I wanted to do was kiss his sweet lips, so I did just that for as long as I was able to keep him there with me.

*****

I stand up, adjusting my leggings around my waistline. "Um, so… you reminded me," I tell Lee hesitantly. "I have some news too."

"Good news or bad? You are making it sound like bad news."

"Uh, yeah… I wouldn't say it's good news, but I guess it all depends on how you look at it."

"Okay, you know what, I will finish telling you my news first, and then you can lay it on me," Lee says.

I nod. "I guess bad news should always go second," I reply.

Although I don't know if I actually think bad news should follow good news. I think I've always decided on hearing good news last whenever someone gave me the option because who wants to be left with a bad taste in their mouth?

Lee grins widely. "You aren't going to believe what I have to tell you."

"Holy cow, just spit it out already," I say impatiently.

"I won!" Lee shouts while jumping into the air. Lee lands with his legs spread, arms above his head, and eyes tilted toward the ceiling—in a star-like position.

"Are you doing yoga?" I ask, confused. It looked like one of those star poses the yoga class does in the room beside where Lee and I do our training sessions.

Lee looks at me in disbelief and flaps his arms back down toward his sides. "I told you I won, and you are focused on a pose you think is from a yoga class?"

"Well, I don't understand. What did you win?"

"Yogurt! For a year!" Lee says excitedly. "You didn't even bother to enter your name into the drawing because you thought there was no chance in Hell they would pick either of our names. Now what do you have to say to that?"

"That's… really great," I respond flatly.

"You're not stoked?" Lee asks. "We can do yogurt two times a week now! It's like the same price because I would still be paying for two yogurts—yours both times. Mine would be free!"

Lee's enthusiasm diminishes as he notices my sad expression. I turn my gaze toward the mat on the ground because I can't bring myself to tell Lee the news while looking him in the eyes. "I'm going to move up North next month," I murmur.

Lee's shoulders drop, his head slumps over, and he looks defeated. "Move up North? But you told me you weren't going to go."

I take a step closer to Lee. "I know—I—please, don't be upset." I place a hand on his shoulder. "It just makes more sense for Ethan's and my relationship. Plus, I won't have to pay rent."

"What do you mean?"

Crap! I forgot I had only mentioned moving closer to Ethan and not in with him.

Lee looks up at me, but now his sadden eyes look fiery in the worst ways. "You are leaving everything—

your job, your sister, nephew, niece… Me. All for some guy you've only been dating for a short time? And it blows my mind that you are going to live with him!"

Lee shoves my hand off his shoulder, and I sadly watch my hand fall back to my side.

I try to explain myself, "Ethan and I dated in high school for a couple of years. It's not like we just met a little while ago."

"Yeah, exactly. He dumped you in high school and left you for the chick who liked to get around. She showed a little bit of interest in Ethan, and then he left you. I told myself I wouldn't say anything, but I don't understand how you could let someone like that back into your life. You deserve better."

Hmm. I guess I somehow pushed that detail of Ethan's and my high school breakup to the back of my mind. Well, now you know the entire story of our breakup, but it doesn't change the fact that I'm still head-over-heels for Ethan. He's different now.

"I know it's not my place to tell you who you should date and who you shouldn't, but I was hoping the whole thing between you and Ethan was just going to be a temporary thing. Can't you see that you aren't supposed to be with Ethan?"

I feel my anger start to rise. Why can't anyone be happy for me? Why is everyone constantly criticizing my relationship with Ethan? Can't they see I'm happy? I just want to be with someone and be happy! But I'm the bad guy here, not Lee. He is my best friend, and I want to keep it that way, even after I leave. I try to fight back the fury that's raging inside of me.

"I can't believe you are telling me this. If I'm not supposed to be with Ethan, then who else?" I look at myself in the mirror and point at my reflection. "Who else is going to want that?" Lee looks over his shoulder to see what I'm pointing at, and I continue, "Who else is going to want to kiss an average girl like me? What other guy wants a future with someone who is a *seven and a half*?" I would probably keep going, but my face is kind of ugly from trying not to cry, and people are starting to stare.

Lee sighs, becoming gentler, and the fierceness in his eyes is no longer present. "Me," he responds softly.

I look at Lee, confused. "Wha—what did you say?"

"Me," he repeats himself. "I told you, I thought you were a seven and a half because you were unrecognizable to me after you changed your appearance, but more importantly, you started to act different, and you weren't the same Zoe I grew up with. Things that shouldn't have mattered meant everything to you." I feel like Lee is trying to pierce my soul with his words as he continues, "I liked the Zoe who used to give me crap for taking forever to do my hair. I've missed the Zoe who was okay with shopping at thrift stores. I want the Zoe who cared more about her fetish with vampire romances rather than her obsession with the newest makeup tutorial, and honestly, if you wanted to chop off all your hair and wear a garbage bag every day, I would still love you for who you were on the inside—just as long as you were the same girl I shared my pork bun with when I first met you. Yeah… that girl, the one who didn't care what other people thought about her glasses or my stinky lunch. That girl, now, she's a ten. Heck! She's off the charts, in my opinion."

I shake my head trying to make sense of what Lee is telling me. This is all so much to take in. "I don't understand," I say. "What are you saying, Lee?" I ask, guarded.

It's clear Lee doesn't like what I've become in my endeavors to become a better version of myself. Is he telling me he has more than just "best friend" feelings for me?

Lee walks toward me—close enough to where his body is two inches from mine. I look up at him, and he says, "I've liked you more than a friend ever since you let me sit by you at lunch."

"What?" I ask, shocked.

Lee continues, "And I *loved* you more than a friend ever since you sat me down on your couch and made me watch *Twilight* with you."

"I—uh," I stammer. "Did you just say you *love* me… more than a friend?" My eyes are wide due to the shock radiating from my body.

"Yes, Zoe. I love you. I'm begging you, don't move in with Ethan. Stay here with me," Lee pleads. "I can make you happy."

My heart feels like it's about to explode with all the anxiety it's just endured, but I'm also fuming inside. Why is Lee telling me this now? Why wait over twenty years to express these feelings, especially when I've found someone I could have a future with.

"Why are you telling me this now?" I ask angrily.

"I was going to tell you the other day, but then Ethan showed up. It killed me hearing about Ethan day in and day out. I wanted to tell you how I felt so many times, but I wasn't sure if it would ruin our friendship. I didn't want to lose you."

My eyes become watery because I know how bad I've hurt my best friend. Is there only an inch between Lee and me now? I can't tell, but it looks like he's closer.

I try to reason with Lee and say, "I don't want to hurt—"

My words are cut off by Lee abruptly wrapping his arms around me and pushing himself against my body. Somehow, his lips have made themselves onto mine, and for whatever reason… it's not weird.

I kiss Lee back, and apparently, kissing other guys doesn't feel the same as kissing Ethan. Or maybe kissing Lee isn't the same as kissing anyone else. Lee's kiss is gentle and loving. I've never felt more comfort in my life.

When Ethan kisses me, he makes me feel desired. But with Lee, I feel—Oh, my gosh! I'm cheating on Ethan!

I push myself away from Lee and look at him, panicked.

"I can't do this," I say and run out of the gym. I quickly get into my car, but before I drive away, I notice Lee still standing in the same spot we shared a kiss.

He looks destroyed because his words weren't able to embed themselves deep enough into my heart.

Chapter Eight

Wrong or Right

I've been trying to get a hold of Lee for the last two weeks. He hasn't answered any of my texts or calls. I've even shown up at his house, but his parents kept telling me he wasn't feeling well and wouldn't let me in. Many times, I had thought about ambushing him at his work, but I thought it might make things worse, and I wouldn't be able to have a conversation with Lee while he's in the middle of a training session.

As I watch the movers drive away from my window in my empty studio, I try not to regret my decision to move in with Ethan. I call Lee one last time and decide to leave him a voicemail before I walk out and begin my new life.

"Hey, Lee… It's me. The worst friend on the planet," I awkwardly chuckle. *"Just wanted to say bye before I leave…*

and, uh, what I really want to say is that I'm sorry. I never wanted to hurt you. I just have to do what I think is best for my future… I really hope I can still have you be a part of it. I want to keep in touch. I can always come visit. You are—"

Lee's phone cuts me off. I've never left a voicemail long enough for that to ever happen. I bet I sounded desperate, which I am. Lee has been my best friend for more than two decades. I feel like I've lost a piece of myself.

I really hope I don't regret my decision. I haven't been able to stop thinking about Lee kissing me. It felt so warm and almost… right. When I was kissing Lee, it seemed like all my worldly worries vanished. It felt like it was meant to be, but I also want to be with Ethan, and Ethan's different now. He's amazing and treats me how a woman should be treated. Plus, Ethan's my first, and he could be my only if I continue to do everything correctly—as long as I continue being his perfect girl.

I walk out and say goodbye to my studio filled with so many memories, knowing deep down, I have lost my best friend.

Story Three

I Want You Forever

Chapter One

Some Surprise

Before Edward Cullen from *Twilight,* there was Tom Welling from that Superman series on TV, and a few years before Tom, there was Brad Pitt. Okay… I know what you are probably thinking—Brad Pitt? Ew. He's used up and old. Brad sometimes looks like a hobo who made a visit to a salon. You know, like a homeless person who takes care of himself, but you know he's still homeless. Anyway, all valid points, but just hear me out. Brad didn't *always* look like that, and once upon a time, he looked pretty yummy shirtless. If you haven't seen *Troy,* let's just say you are missing out.

I begged my mom to subscribe to some magazine. I can't even remember the name. It's been so long. Well, I begged and pleaded for months before my eleventh birthday, hoping my mom would give in and purchase the magazine subscription for my present. I think I drove her crazy because she ended up bending to my wish and put down the money.

I remember one night, just casually flipping through the pages of the magazine that just came in the mail that afternoon. I gasped and started jumping up and down on my bed. I excitedly ripped out the three-page fold-out of Brad lying on his side, dressed in blue jeans—and *only* blue jeans. Brad's skin was lightly covered in dew, and he was smiling at me from some coastal getaway spot. I hung that picture over my headboard, and every night before bed, for three straight years in a row, I kissed him goodnight. Okay, you got me… four years in a row.

Sometimes there would be pictures in the magazines of who was dating who. All the women looked surreal—nothing like the ladies you would see walking down the street or lying on the sand at the beach. These women were perfect—not one flaw—nothing like me.

I sit on a bench with my bag beside me at the airport, continuing to think about my childhood crushes and the women that completed them.

"Hey there, beautiful." Ethan's voice pulls me from my childhood memories. "Everything all right? You looked like you were deep in thought. Thinking about something important?"

I shake my head, stand up, and give Ethan a hug. "No," I reply. "Just happy I'm here with you."

"How was the flight?" Ethan asks. "You don't look like you recently traveled."

"It was a short flight," I respond, although I did do my makeup while I was on the plane, and it did take me the whole hour and a half to beautify myself, which also reminds me of how annoyed I am that TSA confiscated my liquid primer because it was half an ounce over the limit allowed. I paid twenty bucks for that stuff!

"I have a surprise for you waiting at my place—our place," Ethan says. "I should probably get used to calling it *our* place now."

"I like the sound of that," I say. "And I must admit, you really know how to treat a girl—spoiling me rotten almost every time I see you."

As we drive to Ethan's place, I notice the paved streets are transforming into unrefined dirt roads, and the tropical palms are being replaced by tall spruce-like trees.

I've only been camping once with Lee's family, but that was at the beach. I imagine this is what "real" camping would look like as I peer out the window.

We pull up to Ethan's house. My eyes widen with surprise, and now I hardly miss my studio.

"I know it's not much," Ethan says, putting his car in park. "And probably not what you were expecting terrain-wise."

Ethan was right. I wasn't expecting to be living next to Yogi Bear. I guess I thought Ethan would be living closer to the Bay Area or near a big city. The rural living space looks beautiful, but it will take some getting used to.

I slowly unbuckle my seatbelt, admiring the cabin-like structure. "So, you like what you see so far?" he asks.

I look at him like I just won a new car. "I love it."

Although, I begin to wonder just how far the coast is from Ethan's house. I guess I should've asked these questions before I decided to move in with him, not that it would've hindered my decision. Lee would always make fun of my weak arms whenever we went paddle boarding anyway, which was once a year when he practically dragged me to do something besides lounging on the couch. Still, those will always be great memories in my book.

"Well, hopefully, you'll love the inside too. I had to hire an interior designer because I have no sense of style when it comes to furnishing a home."

Ethan unlocks the door to *our* home and says, "Welcome to your new place."

"Can I just say," I mention, "if I knew you lived in such a nice place like this, I wouldn't have needed so much verbal convincing."

Ethan chuckles. I'm glad he thinks I was joking about the whole convincing me thing. "Yeah, I guess it is a nice cabin in the woods," Ethan says, being modest.

"More like a resort," I murmur.

"Let me take you to your surprise."

I throw my bag on the floor, eager to find out what's awaiting me. Ethan grabs my hand and leads me to the kitchen, which is amazing, by the way. There's so much counter space, and there's not just a fruit basket and microwave lining the counter like in most homes. Ethan has some kind of fancy espresso machine as well as a bunch of other gadgets I'm not too familiar with. The light bounces off the shiny appliances that look untouched.

"So, as you know," Ethan says, "I'm not big on cooking since I'm so busy, but I went ahead and ordered everything you could possibly need. I wanted to make your life easier."

Oh… I don't know if Ethan's "thoughtfulness" is going to make my life any easier. Hopefully, he saved all the manuals. Might take me a year to figure out all the "machinery" in his kitchen.

Ethan walks over to a large rectangular-looking box that has two dispensers—one for candy and one for… who knows what.

"I also remembered how you told me you like to eat frozen yogurt, so I bought a frozen yogurt machine." Ethan grins widely. "This one is top-of-the-line. You can't get a better one unless we make room for a commercial-grade machine."

Oh, so that's what this thing is for, making yogurt. Doesn't look anything like the ones at the fro-yo shop. How was I supposed to know?

I fake a smile and nod my head. "Mhmm.... So cool," I lie. Now I'm thinking of Lee again. Lovely.

"We can watch a movie tonight. I can order takeout, too, since you had to fly this afternoon and are probably exhausted. We can eat popcorn and have some yogurt for dessert," Ethan says, a little too enthusiastically, but I don't blame him. After all, he won't be the one making the popcorn and yogurt.

I bet you are thinking I sound ungrateful. I guess I should be happy I don't have to make dinner. Actually, you know what? If I'm being honest, I think I'm kind of peeved that Ethan bought all these things for me to make food and drinks with, or maybe I'm just being ridiculous. It's not like he bought me a vacuum as a gift. I think some would say that it's close enough. I don't know. I guess I'll just go with it. Ethan had good intentions with his kitchen purchases. I will give him the benefit of the doubt.

Anyway, I bet the movie we watch won't be *Twilight*, and I bet the fro-yo won't taste as good. I thought I was missing Lee when he was ignoring me, but now I really miss him—like a bun missing its pork. I wonder if Lee will ever forgive me, or if I can ever forgive myself for what I did to Lee.

Too many thoughts are winding uncontrollably through my head. I take a deep breath and reassure myself. Well, at least nothing can go wrong with Ethan, right?

Wrong.

This is the story of how I thought I would be alone forever.

Chapter Two

No Flame

Six months have passed since I've moved in with Ethan. I've been going a little stir crazy, staying in most of the time. Ethan eventually let his housekeeper go because he felt like I was "handling" the upkeep fine on my own.

And five months ago, I had given up on calling and texting Lee. I'm positive he blocked my number anyway.

I glance at the clock as I duplicate one of those thirty-minute meals I had seen Rachel Ray whip up on The Food Channel. It's already been over thirty minutes, by the way—forty-two minutes, if you want to be exact. I grab a pair of tongs and remove the sliced chicken breast from the sizzling pan, turn the heat down, and walk over to the pantry to retrieve the flour—similar routine to what I've been doing every night for the last… however many days.

It seems like my life has been on repeat for too long. Don't get me wrong, Ethan still holds my heart. He still spoils and satisfies me emotionally and physically. He even bought me some gym equipment, so now I have my own personal gym in one of the spare bedrooms. Ethan never neglects me, but something feels off. Maybe I'm just homesick. It seems like an eternity since I've seen Trish and the kiddos.

"Honey, I'm home!" Ethan says. Also, the same thing he says every night when he returns from work. "Something burning?"

I look down at my gravy. It's boiling and crustifying on the sides of the pan. "Holy mother of cows!"

I quickly turn off the burner and hold up the pan away from the heat. I got distracted, reminiscing about my new life. I set the pan down on the counter and cringe at my cooking mistake.

"I hope you are okay with chicken and potatoes without gravy," I say, disappointed.

Ethan shrugs. "Better than a TV dinner."

I bite the inside of my cheek, mad at myself. "Sorry."

Ethan smiles. "Oh, no. Don't apologize. I didn't mean it like that. I'm sure it will taste just as good without the gravy."

I bring our dinner to the table. "Did you guys finally figure out all the coding today?" I ask.

"Not quite, but the team is almost there. I can feel it! I think by next week, it will be smooth sailing, and we will be able to complete the project by the end of the year."

I nod my head as I cut into my chicken. My mind is elsewhere, thinking of what I'm missing in SoCal.

"I think everyone can use a good break this weekend," Ethan continues. "No one's doing any overtime. Heck, I think I can use a break. TGIF."

Oh, yeah. Today is Friday, isn't it? My days tend to blur together, but I guess it's normal to lose track of the days when you don't get out much.

Oh… and I guess that means we will be watching another documentary tonight. Ethan has a thing about documentaries, and it doesn't matter what kind of documentary either. The one about some wife feeding her husband to the lions wasn't terrible, but the one about some creeper neighbor abducting a little girl next door to him was the worst. When I watch a movie or a show, I want to laugh or imagine I'm the girl getting swept off her feet. I don't want to be afraid of every man I see when I make a shopping run, thinking I could be his next victim.

"There's this documentary one of my employees was telling me about," Ethan says. "It's about a guy who satisfies his homicidal desires by becoming a contract killer for—"

I stop listening to Ethan's synopsis. It sounds like I might have nightmares for at least two days or maybe two weeks after watching the documentary Ethan's talking about.

"Hey," I interrupt. "Uh, what would you say to switching it up tonight?"

"Oh, yeah, yeah," Ethan responds. "We can do that. What did you want to do? I can go grab us some pastries or actual ice cream if you don't want frozen yogurt. You know how I like ice cream better than frozen yogurt anyway."

First of all, ice cream is not better than frozen yogurt! I like the icy texture rather than the creaminess of ice cream. Or maybe I just find fro-yo to be more comforting since that's the only thing Lee and I ever got. Lee's stomach couldn't handle a bunch of dairy. He told me it was pretty common in Asians, and frozen yogurt is easier on his digestive system. Since we usually went back to my studio after getting fro-yo, I never complained. I didn't need Lee blowing up the pipes.

"Actually, I was referring to the documentary," I explain.

"It doesn't sound interesting to you?" Ethan asks.

"Uh, I mean it does," I lie. "But I was thinking maybe we could watch a movie tonight… or something."

Ethan looks disappointed, but he's also always understanding. One of the best things about him is that if

I'm really set on something or have other desires, he is always willing to compromise.

"Um, okay," Ethan responds. "I wouldn't mind watching something different tonight if that's what you want."

I grin widely and clap my hands. "Yay!"

"What did you have in mind?" Ethan asks. "Oh, did you want to watch that one romantic comedy about the…" Ethan really has to think back to when I was telling him about this movie. "The Asian chef that's lonely? I think you said she goes back to her hometown and rekindles a spark with her ex or something? What is it called? *Always Be My…. Ah,* I can't remember," he admits.

I chuckle. "I'm surprised you remembered that much of what I told you," I joke.

"Hey!" Ethan shouts. "You don't give me enough credit. I know you think I don't listen, but I do."

That movie did catch my interest, but I also haven't seen *Twilight* in forever. "I was actually thinking of something along the lines of… romance and vampires if that's not too farfetched for you."

"I can do vampires, but vampires and romance? I've never heard of such a thing."

Uh… really? I'm pretty sure *Twilight* isn't the only vampire romance out there. It's the best, but definitely not the only.

"Well, you are in for a treat," I say happily.

*****

We are at the part in the movie where Edward reveals himself to Bella in the sunlight—diamond-like skin and all.

"I thought vampires can't go into the sunlight," Ethan says and then shoves a handful of popcorn into his mouth.

"These ones can," I explain.

"Hmm… that's weird," he says. "I'm pretty sure they are supposed to ignite when in the sun and turn to ash."

But he's wrong. There's nothing *weird* about the best movie on the planet. I take a handful of popcorn as well and ignore Ethan's comment and lack of knowledge about vampires.

We are silent up until the baseball scene, but I have to express my feelings toward this part of the movie. "Okay, so, this is one of my all-time favorite parts of the movie," I say, staring intently at the TV. "It pretty much has all the feels," I say. "It's the best. It's just amazing."

I look over at Ethan, wondering why he isn't responding. Ethan's head has flopped back onto the couch, his eyes are shut, and he's mouth breathing like he always does.

I'm annoyed.

How could Ethan fall asleep while the most awesome movie is playing? Many times, I've had to pry my eyelids open on Friday nights while trying to make it through a two to three-hour documentary.

I sigh, bummed. I suppose we won't be watching any more of the *Twilight* series.

I really miss my best friend.

Chapter Three

Napa Valley

"I've been dying for a getaway," I tell Ethan as I shove a couple of changes of clothes into my overnight bag.

I peek over at Ethan, who is neatly folding each article of clothing into his suitcase. "I wish I could take you on a longer trip, but you know how it is with the project going on at work."

I nod my head. It's not like I could afford to go on *any* getaway *before* I started seeing Ethan. "I just can't wait to find out where you are taking me," I say excitedly. "Now, be honest… should I pack a bathing suit?"

"The answer will always be no," Ethan smirks.

We drive about an hour and a half further up North. Ethan has held my hand the entire drive. He was only able to do this because his car is an automatic. It reminds me of the time Lee attempted to teach me how to drive his car, which is a stick.

"I really don't feel like it's necessary to know how to drive a stick shift," I said to Lee as I buckled up, preparing for my unwanted driving lesson.

"You sound so naive right now," Lee said, annoyed.

I glared at him and ran my hand down my braid because I was getting anxious. I never really enjoyed driving, but Lee always made me pick him up and drive him places because he was convinced the more I drove, the more comfortable I would become. To be honest, the more I drove, the more crazy stuff I witnessed on the roads, which just made things worse.

"How is that naive?" I murmured.

"Well, a good example is an apocalypse."

My eyebrows scrunched as I thought of how Lee's example was ridiculous. "Really?" I asked, not convinced. "An apocalypse?"

"Yeah, say there's a zombie apocalypse, and you are getting chased by a hoard of the undead. You see a car in the distance, so you run a half-mile to the vehicle to make your getaway to save your life. As you approach the car, you are out of breath, and the zombies are closing in. They aren't the super crazy fast kind of zombies. They are kind of slow, but not too slow. You know, kind of like medium speed, or I don't know if I would say medium—"

"Okay!" I shouted. "I get it. The zombies are close. Continue."

"Jeez. You don't have to yell," Lee said. "So, anyway, you get to the car and hop in, and you spend a whole forty-five seconds looking for the keys, which you finally find hidden in the visor… I would've looked there first, but I know you wouldn't."

I slapped Lee on the side of his shoulder. He laughed and continued, "You finally put the key into the ignition, look down to put the car in drive, and realize the car is useless in your hands because you don't know how to drive… that's right… a stick."

I pursed my lips. "That will never happen. Where do you come up with these things?"

"I just like to be prepared, is all," Lee said. "Now start up The Lady."

Yeah, so, Lee nicknamed his car "The Lady." I never understood why guys always referred to cars as girls. How come they couldn't be boys? I also thought Asian men were supposed to be into computer games and collecting comic books rather than cars or whatever. I guess maybe I was naive *in that sense.*

Anyway, I started up the car like Lee instructed. My driving lesson ended before it began because Lee couldn't handle me grinding the clutch every five seconds. I guess he didn't think I was going to be that terrible of a student, but I was.

We switched seats, and Lee drove me home. "So, what's going to happen if I don't know how to drive a stick and there is an actual apocalypse?" I asked.

Lee looked over at me and grinned. "I guess you will have to make sure you *stick* with me. I won't let the zombies eat your brains."

"You are such a dork," I said, laughing, but I knew there was some honesty to what Lee was saying. He would take a bullet for me, or better yet, sacrifice his brains for mine.

"I won't make you close your eyes this time," Ethan says as we drive by what seems to be thousands of rows of grapevines. "And I hope you like white wine. I know I never really keep anything in the alcohol cabinet at home."

I was actually kind of bummed when I first discovered where Ethan's alcohol cabinet was. All it housed was some margarita mix, but it made sense because I'm pretty sure Ethan's dad liked to hit the booze before noon almost every day. Ethan mentioned something about how addictive personalities are passed down to children. I don't know if I really believed what he said, but I guess I understood where he was coming from. When we stayed at the resort the first time I visited him, I wondered why Ethan only allotted himself one glass of champagne. If I were to guess, he probably had the same limitations for this trip.

"Are you planning on getting me drunk this weekend and taking advantage of me?" I ask Ethan.

"Why would you assume such a thing?" Ethan asks with a sly look in his eyes.

"Well, are you planning on limiting your alcohol intake like the last time we 'shared' a bottle?"

"One glass per night for me," Ethan replies.

"Okay, so, yeah, that's a lot of wine that will be left over for me."

"Is that a complaint?" Ethan jokes.

"No, I guess not."

"And you know I don't have to get you drunk for you to let me take advantage of you, which by the way, is what I plan on doing with you tonight."

I shake my head at Ethan's comment, but let's be realistic, what Ethan says is true.

The next morning, I quickly roll out of bed and shower before Ethan wakes up. I try to make myself as presentable as possible before Ethan can get a glimpse of me. I bet this is what Beyonce felt like every time she dated a new person before she met Jay-Z—having no choice but to remove her weave and makeup in front of her dates. It's logical, right? I mean, I'm not the only chick on the planet who prefers her lover *not* to see her with ratted hair and smudged mascara from the night before. Plus, I can't help but think about that one time Ethan referred to me as that slimy monster. The last thing

I need for Ethan to witness is me rolling out of bed a mess. I can imagine him saying, "Wow, Zoe, you almost gave me a heart attack. I barely recognized you. You look like you stuck your finger into a wall socket and got electrocuted." Yeah, I don't dare let those words leave Ethan's mouth, so that's why I try to prevent giving him that option.

"I'm surprised you got up so early after last night," Ethan says, finally waking up and stretching his arms into the air.

"Yeah, I'm just about done getting ready," I reply.

"That's good," Ethan says. "Because I have the best day planned for us. Oh, and happy anniversary, beautiful."

My reflection in the mirror smiles back at me as I hear Ethan's compliment, and I finish putting on my lipstick.

"Is this attire fitting for today's adventures?" I ask Ethan while walking out of the bathroom. I run my hands from the top of my chest to the bottom of my dress, putting my outfit on display. "Do you like?" I ask.

Ethan sits up, exposing his perfect, unclothed upper body. He nods his head multiple times. "Uh-huh," Ethan says like he's dumbfounded.

The only thing that would make this ensemble better would be bigger boobs, I think to myself.

Ethan looks at the clock on the nightstand. "You know, we still have a couple of hours before brunch."

Ethan anxiously grabs the sheet and yanks it off him. "Come over here," he says seductively. "We still have some time."

I walk over to the bed, but instead of straddling him, I sit down beside him. "I don't want to ruin my makeup," I tell him and gently give him a peck, so I don't smudge my lipstick.

Ethan sighs, disappointed. "Fine. I guess I can wait until tonight."

Ethan heads to the shower, and I flip on the TV as he gets ready. How come resorts never have anything good to choose from? You always have to overpay for a mediocre movie if you want to be entertained.

After scrolling through the same options more than twice, I give up and opt for watching a new makeup tutorial on my phone. I unlock my screen and cover my mouth with my hand, completely and utterly in shock.

"Lee?" I gasp.

"What's that?" Ethan shouts from the shower.

"Uh… nothing!" I yell and anxiously open the message.

Lee texted me. I can't believe I have a text from Lee after all this time. It reads: "*Hey, it's been a long time. Was just eating some fro-yo and thought of you.*"

Lee was eating frozen yogurt and thought of me? I reread the text over again, trying to understand what it *actually* meant. There's no way it actually means what it says, right? Does this mean he forgives me, and we can be friends again? Does this mean he misses me? Maybe his feelings toward me have changed. I don't know.

I text him back: "*It's really good to hear from you. How are you and your family?*"

My leg is bouncing up and down involuntarily, impatiently waiting for a response.

Lee finally replies: "*I've been good. Family's been good. My grandma and mom miss you a lot. They wanted me to ask if you plan on visiting any time soon.*"

I can't help but feel like this text needs some deciphering, but I can't seem to figure out any underlying meanings. I wonder if Lee's family were the ones who convinced him to finally text me. If not that, then what made Lee decide to reach out after almost a year?

"*I don't know when, but I want to. I miss everyone,*" I reply.

I hear Ethan turn off the water, and I quickly close my messages and toss my phone into my purse. I tuck my palms under my thighs, lean over to peer through the open bathroom door, and smile at Ethan to show him I've been patiently waiting for him while he was getting ready.

Wait, why should I feel weird about Lee texting me? Why do I feel like I just did something I shouldn't, like I have just done something sneaky? Is it because I've kept Lee's true feelings toward me locked away in a vault? Maybe I should tell Ethan now? But it might ruin our trip, and Ethan may never want to see me again if I tell him about Lee's and my kiss. Yeah, maybe I should come clean and remove this weight off my shoulders—no, it's fine. It's not like I was the one who made the first move, Lee did, and, I mean, what's the point? It was so long ago. There's no sense in bringing it up now.

"Want to take a walk through the vineyards before brunch?" Ethan asks, wrapping a towel around his waist.

"That sounds super-duper," I say.

"Super-duper?" Ethan asks, confused.

"Uh, yeah. Super… D-duper." I add a little arm gesture to go with my saying. I think most people swing their arm like I just did when they say, "shucks" or something along those lines.

Ethan squints at me. "You're acting kind of strange. I don't think I've ever heard you say super-duper before," he mentions. "Is everything all right?"

I chuckle awkwardly. "Yeah, um… just excited for our day," I lie.

I take a deep breath and tell myself to stop thinking about Lee, his feelings for me, and the not-so-friendly kiss we shared before I left San Diego.

The sky is the perfect shade of blue today. Ethan holds my hand as we walk down a path lined by never-ending grapevines, and as I look ahead, there's nothing but acres of vineyard and the rolling California hills in the background.

My stomach growls loudly, and I place my hand over the spot where the noise came from.

Ethan looks at me and smiles. "We are almost there, and our brunch will be waiting for us. In fact, we ought to hurry. It looks like we are running a little late now. I forgot how slow you walk."

I look around, confused. "Where's the restaurant?" I ask.

Ethan points his finger toward the sky. "Look up."

I tilt my head back and see about a dozen hot air balloons dancing just below the clouds. "Oh, wow," I say, still transfixed on the vibrant colored balloons in the sky. "I've never seen anything like this."

Ethan looks back at me. "Are you excited?"

"Huh?" I ask.

"To go on a hot air balloon ride," Ethan replies.

I look at him and laugh like he just made a joke, and Ethan looks at me like I've asked a dumb question.

"Oh… you mean, you are serious," I respond, quickly wiping the smile off my face and clear my throat. "Uh, yeah… I'm excited," I lie. "I've never been on a hot air balloon ride before."

I guess I never mentioned to Ethan I'm scared of heights. Okay, not just scared, like when someone sees a spider. I'm deathly afraid of heights. My toes get tingly when I have to climb the step stool to reach cans on the top shelf in Ethan's pantry.

I start to have a flashback to when Lee and I were eight, and his dad built him a treehouse in his backyard. I remember the construction looked durable, but I wasn't convinced a house should be in a tree.

"Come on, Zoe," Lee said, trying to encourage me to join him inside the treehouse. Lee leaned over the edge and waved his hand toward me.

I looked at the rope ladder hesitantly. "Uh, I don't know. I kind of feel like playing in the sandbox today," I replied and walked over to the open sandbox we hadn't played in for months and shuffled my feet in the sand.

"You don't want to play in there," Lee suggested. "My mom hasn't checked for weeks to see if Cassie pooped in the sand."

Cassie was Lee's cat who roamed the block. She was more wild than tame. His parents left food and water on the porch for her, and she came and went as she pleased.

I looked down at the sand and noticed there was something beside my foot that resembled a cat turd. I quickly hopped out of the sandbox and instantly regretted wearing sandals.

"Just wait until you see the inside of the treehouse. You are going to flip!" Lee shouted.

I placed my hand on one of the rope rungs, which happened to be my only way up to join Lee. My heart started to beat frantically. "I—uh, I don't know if I can do this, Lee," I said, frightened.

"You don't need to be scared," Lee encouraged me. "If I can do it, you can too."

"I'm scared I might fall," I admitted.

"Just keep looking up at me," Lee said. "As long as you keep looking at me, you won't fall."

Lee continued to lean over the edge and kept waving his hand for me to climb up the ladder.

"Okay… um, here goes nothing," I said and began making my way up.

Once I got my feet off the ground, the rope began to sway in the wind.

"Remember, keep looking at me," Lee reminded me.

I looked up at his chubby but confident face. "I'm doing it!" I yelled.

"Good!" Lee shouted. "You're doing good, and you're almost halfway there."

"I am?" I asked excitedly, but then I made the mistake of looking down.

"No! No!" Lee screamed. "Don't look down. You are supposed to keep looking at me."

I froze and closed my eyes. My heart was knocking hard against my chest, and my fingers and toes felt numb. It didn't matter how hard I gripped onto the rope, I knew I was going to fall, which is exactly what happened.

The next thing I knew, I was on the ground, and Lee was yelling for his mom. I felt Lee place his hand on the back of my head, propping it up. Lee's mom was running toward me, dressed in one of her red aprons. She had a wooden spoon in one hand and a towel in the other.

Anyway, it was nothing to be too concerned about. Turned out I didn't even have a concussion or anything, seeing as I was only about three feet from the ground, but I did sprain my pinky finger and had to wear one of those metal splints for a few weeks until it healed.

After that happened, Lee's mom demanded her husband take down the treehouse and reassemble it on the ground. Lee's dad did just that, right next to Cassie's "litter box."

Lee and I made a lot of memories in that treehouse. I remember we used to carve little sayings on the wooden planks inside. Lee's favorites were some cheesy lines he came up with. My favorite was our initials that we carved under the saying "FFL" as in, friends for life. I wonder if Lee remembers the pact we made when we carved that promise into the treehouse.

"I heard it's the best experience," Ethan mentions. "Let's go." He tugs on my arm and encourages me to walk faster, and now we're almost jogging. "Our wine is going to go bad with you walking like a tortoise."

The empty field seemed to appear out of nowhere. I thought Ethan and I were going to be lost in the vineyards forever, or at least, that's what I hoped for if it meant avoiding soaring through the air.

The first thing I notice is the romantic brunch placed neatly inside the basket.

"Welcome, Mr. and Mrs. Jennings," the man says who is standing by the balloon. "It's a pleasure to meet you both. My name is Ben."

"Oh, um, we aren't," I try to correct the tour guide and awkwardly point to Ethan and then myself. "We aren't—"

"My apologies," Ben says. "I shouldn't have assumed."

"It's all right," Ethan responds. "Close enough."

Okay, I guess I will just go with the flow on this one. Apparently, Ben can call us Sonny and Cher for all Ethan's concerned.

"Shall we?" Ben asks, gesturing toward the basket.

Pins and needles pierce the ends of my toes and slowly creep up higher along the bottom of my feet and then to my legs. There's a panic in my chest, and I'm frozen like the frightened child who was hanging onto the rope ladder years ago.

"I—I, uh—" I stammer and close my eyes tightly.

"Are you all right?" Ethan whispers into my ear.

"Uh, Ben. Just give us a minute, would you?" Ethan says.

I manage to nod my head, but my eyes are still glued shut. I can feel Ethan position his body in front of me and place both of his hands on the sides of my shoulders.

"You're shaking like you just got out of a cold shower," Ethan mentions and tries to comfort me. "You have to let me know what's going on, or I can't help."

Ethan waits another moment and says, "How about we start by you opening your eyes and letting me hold your hand." He gently rubs my arms.

I swallow deeply and find the courage to open my eyes.

"Oh, is something wrong with your hand?" Ethan asks.

I hadn't realized until now, but I had been gripping my pinky finger with my other hand.

"Just an old injury," I explain.

I slowly release my finger from my protective grip and place my hand in Ethan's.

"Are you scared of heights?" Ethan asks.

I nod my head.

"You know I will never let you fall," Ethan says, smiling warmly.

My heart calms. I let out an awkward chuckle. "I know… I just— had this terrible experience when I was little. I, um, I fell off this rope ladder." I tuck a loose strand of hair behind my ear and look down at the ground, embarrassed.

Ethan places his finger underneath my chin and tilts my head up to meet his gaze. "There's no need to be embarrassed. We can have our brunch on the ground if that's what you want to do."

I wipe my sweaty palms on the side of my dress and think for a moment. I don't want to ruin his plans. Even though Ethan seemed understanding, I know he would be upset. Ethan wouldn't show me his disappointment, but I mean, even I would be a little peeved if I paid all this money to go on a fancy hot air balloon ride.

"I'm sorry I didn't tell you about my fear sooner," I tell Ethan.

"Don't be. It's not like I ever planned a hike to a top of a mountain or wanted to go rock climbing. Hence, there was never a time for something like that to be brought up." Ethan looks at Ben and says, "Well, looks like we are going to stay on the ground today."

"You sure? There's a brilliant view waiting for you both," Ben replies. "And unfortunately, I won't be able to refund what you've paid for the tour."

"Yeah, I think we will enjoy our brunch on the—"

I decide to be brave today, or maybe the pins and needles have traveled to my brain, numbing my fear. "No," I say, determined. "We should do this."

"What? You're positive you want to?" Ethan asks.

I take a deep breath and respond, "Yes! I can do it. It was such a long time ago—the ladder scenario. Plus, you said you would keep me safe," I say confidently.

Ethan grins. "That's correct. I will never let anything or anyone ever hurt you."

"Okay," I say and step into the basket. Thankfully, Ethan is still holding my hand.

"You won't regret it!" Ben shouts and closes the basket door behind him. Ben releases the balloon into the air with the flame scorching above us, fueling the balloon.

We stand in the very center of the basket, and Ethan wraps his arms around me. "Just look at me if you are nervous," he says, and it reminds me of Lee telling me to stay focused on him as I climbed the ladder to the treehouse. I stare into Ethan's eyes and try not to think of floating off into the sky.

"You are doing great," Ethan says encouragingly. "I'm so proud of you."

I stand in Ethan's arms, trying to tell myself I'm not hundreds of feet from safety. "Thanks," I say quietly.

"I'm going to let go of you in a few minutes," Ethan mentions. "But before I do, I want to tell you how happy you've made me this past year." I continue to look at Ethan's swoony eyes. I don't want to make the same mistake again and look down or even around us. "You are the most beautiful girl I've ever encountered. You take such good care of me. I don't know what I would do if you hadn't given me a second chance. Whenever I'm away from you, you are all I ever want."

For a minute, I don't feel so high up in the atmosphere. Ethan's words are causing my anxiety to disappear.

"I am madly in love with you. I don't think it would be possible for me to live without you."

"I love you too," I manage to say and smile.

"All right," Ethan says and begins to slowly release me from his embrace. "I'm going to let go of you for a moment."

I continue to fixate my gaze on Ethan, and I'm still doing okay. Just as long as I keep looking into Ethan's eyes, I will be okay.

"So, what do you say, Zoe? Will you spend the rest of your days with me?"

I blink my eyes about ten times within five seconds, and then I look down. I realize Ethan is down on his knee, holding an engagement ring. Holy mother of all cows! I was not expecting this. My heart starts to race again, and my whole body is becoming numb.

"Uh, I—um, I—" I stutter.

Now I realize I'm staring out the basket at the wondrous view, but instead of admiring its beauty, my head becomes fuzzy. Instead of enjoying the clouds, my brain feels light and fluffy. I place my hand on my forehead and use my other one to brace myself against the side of the basket. My vision becomes infected with black splotches. I feel Ethan's and Ben's hands grab my arms for support as I slide into a seated position.

"I'm going to land the balloon right now," Ben says urgently.

"No, no," I say, unclearly. My speech is slowed and almost mute. "We haven't eaten those muffins." I point to what I think are yummy baked delights.

"Those aren't muffins," Ethan replies. "Um," Ethan gingerly pushes the top of my arm, causing it to lower to my side. "You are pointing at our guide's… uh—"

"At what?" I ask faintly and try to grab one of the muffins to show Ethan he is wrong. I graze the muffin with the tip of my fingers, but somehow, they seemed to have moved farther away from my grasp.

Ethan mumbles, "Ben's stuff."

"Stuff? What's stuff?"

"Stuff as in junk," Ethan explains.

I blink a few more times and squint hard. "Are you sure they aren't blueberry muff—" Black spots make a comeback, and I close my eyes and lean my head back onto the basket.

"We need to get you on the ground. No exceptions," Ethan says firmly.

"We'll be landing soon," Ben adds. "Just a few more minutes. We are getting lower as we speak."

I feel more at ease and less light-headed knowing this.

The flame under the balloon is extinguished, and I can finally think more clearly.

"Do you need me to call an ambulance, just in case?" Ben asks.

"No, I'm fine," I reply. I stand myself up, ecstatic to have made it safely back down. I grin widely to show Ben and Ethan I'm okay. "See, as long as we aren't flying through the air, I will be just fine." I stare at Ben's shorts for a few seconds too long. They are blue like the color of blueberries. I look at the uneaten food. There aren't any muffins. Darn. "I think I will feel even better after we eat some brunch," I mention.

"Maybe we should take the food back to the room," Ethan suggests.

"No, I rather eat it out here, in the fresh air. Then we can relax for a little before our walk back," I reply.

"That actually might be a good idea," Ethan says.

"I agree," Ben adds. "Take a few minutes before heading back to your room. If you need anything, I will hang out just over there." Ben points to the little outpost the tour guides use, about fifty yards away. Ben gives us a salute and jogs off to give us some privacy.

"You about gave me a heart attack," Ethan says. He holds my hand as we take a seat inside the basket and enjoy our brunch.

"I really thought I was going to be able to go along with it—overly confident, I guess," I chuckle, still a little embarrassed.

"I'm proud of you for trying," Ethan mentions.

I smirk but also feel ashamed of my fear.

Ethan can tell my demeanor has switched since I got all light-headed, so he changes the focus on our food. "Looks like they prepared some five-star sandwiches for us," he says.

"Yeah, looks really great. Way better than what I make at home."

"Well, if yours were just as good, then this brunch wouldn't be as special, right?" Ethan adds as he hands me the sandwich he just unwrapped.

"I am starving," I say just before bringing the artisan sandwich up to my face for a heaping bite. The fresh bread smells like it was baked just this morning. As I begin to sink my teeth into the sandwich, I pause mid-bite and stare at the massive diamond on my left hand.

"Everything all right?" Ethan asks.

I quickly finish taking my bite and chew quickly.

"What's wrong?" Ethan asks impatiently. "Are you feeling light-headed again?"

I shake my head, still trying to mash up the food in my mouth.

"Do you need me to take you to the hospital?"

"No, no," I say with a mouthful.

"Did you say no?" Ethan asks, unsure of my jumbled words. "Maybe I should call somconc and havc a doctor take a look at you." Ethan takes out his phone from his pocket.

I finally swallow and shout, "No!"

Ethan slowly puts his phone away.

"Sorry, no. I'm fine."

"Then what's going on?"

I think about taking another heaping bite out of my sandwich, so I have time to think about how I want to approach this situation. I'm positive I hadn't said yes when we were up in the air, or maybe I did. I don't know. I look down at the ring.

"It's really beautiful," I tell Ethan.

"Oh, I hope you don't mind," Ethan replies. "Just as I took the ring out of the box, you looked like you were about to faint. I already stuck the box back into my pocket, and I slid the ring onto your finger so I could help brace you."

Ethan's explanation seems weird but logical, I suppose. Why do I need to think about it so much anyway? This is what I wanted.

"If you prefer, I can take it off and ask you properly again, and then I can put it back on your finger."

Yes, this is what I wanted and still want. I want to be Ethan's girl.

I shake my head. "No, we don't need to do that. I heard everything you said before I almost fainted." I lean over and gently touch Ethan's cheek before kissing him.

Yeah, I'm Ethan's girl now. I know fireworks should be exploding inside of me, and my mind should be traveling through Ethan's and my future. I should be thinking about what our wedding day will be like and where we will travel on our honeymoon, but for some reason, I can't help but think of Lee.

Chapter Four

Miss You

The next day, after returning from our weekend vacation, it was back to our normal schedule. Ethan headed to work in the morning after I made us breakfast, but before starting on my chores around the house, I decide to facetime Trish to tell her the good news.

"Hey!" Trish shouts excitedly. "I was wondering how long you were going to make me wait between our facetime sessions."

"Are you walking around your living room, dusting?" I ask.

"Not really. I'm just sprucing up the house a little," Trish replies.

"Your house doesn't need dusting three times a day."

"Please, I do not dust my house three times a day."

"You're always in denial. Anyway, yeah, I'm a terrible sister. I should've called you sooner," I admit and notice Ashely and Travis playing in the background. "And, apparently, I'm a terrible Auntie," I say. "This sucks. I miss you guys. The kids have gotten so big in just a year. I feel like I've missed out on so much already."

"Time flies," Trish says. "Pretty soon Travis is going to be taller than me."

"Yeah, it's crazy," I mention.

"So, how are things going living with Ethan?" Trish asks.

I sigh. "It's… okay," I reply. "It's nothing like San Diego. I don't know if I'm really digging the forest scene. I mean, I knew there were redwoods in California, but I never thought I'd be living in a cabin in the woods. It just doesn't quite feel like home."

"Well, it's not *really* a cabin," Trish says while rolling her eyes. "And if you must call it a cabin, it's the most gosh-darn fancy cabin I've ever seen."

"I know, I shouldn't complain. I just miss being close to you and the family."

Trish takes a moment away from dusting and plops down onto her couch. "We miss you too, Zoe."

"Maybe it's not so much the atmosphere I'm not fond of. Maybe it's my lack of excitement. I feel like I'm stuck in a rut. It's the same thing every day—cook, clean, cook, clean, and once in a while, pick up groceries. I also feel like there's no one here I can talk to. Besides Ethan, there's the salesclerk I try to chat it up with once a week. I'm pretty sure he's just out of high school. I bet he thinks I'm too old to converse with. He doesn't say much, but he also reeks of weed. I think he's high, like, all the time." I sigh, bummed. "It's impossible for me to make friends here."

"Okay, well, so much for not complaining," Trish laughs.

Now I feel like an ungrateful house guest. Plus, Trish probably knows what it's like to have the same routine every day. Maybe that's just how it is when you are in a serious relationship. Maybe I should just get used to it and stop acting like a whiny baby.

"Just forget I said anything," I reply.

"I'm just giving you a hard time! You know you can talk to me about anything. Why don't you visit us?" Trish suggests. "The kids need some time with their Auntie, and it's not healthy to keep yourself cooped up in the house."

"I should," I say but also remember that I haven't been "cooped up" entirely. Ethan did take me on a nice vacation this last weekend. "Oh!" I yell. "How could I have forgotten." I grin and pause.

"What?" Trish asks impatiently. "Tell me now."

"Well…" I stall for anticipation.

Then I quickly shoot my hand up in front of the phone to show off my ring.

Trish places her hand over her mouth and gasps. The feed on my phone blurs as Trish jumps up and down. "Oh, my gosh!" she yells. "I can't believe it!"

I let my hand relax at my side. "I know. Me either," I reply. "One minute Ethan's proposing, and the next, my finger has a ring on it," I chuckle. "What do you know."

"Tell me all about how he asked," Trish demands.

"It was really amazing. Well, kind of. I mean, the trip was amazing. Ethan took me to a winery in Napa Valley. We stayed in a fancy resort, drank lots of wine—well, I did. Ate lots of yummy food, and—"

"And did the nasty all day and night?"

"Holy cow, Trish. Can you not? What I was going to say was, and got engaged."

"Oh, whatever. So, what do you mean *kind of*?" Trish asks, confused. "Every aspect sounds like the best vacation."

"Ninety-nine percent of the trip was perfect… except the part where I almost fainted."

"Oh, no. What happened?"

"Ethan planned a hot air balloon ride," I explain.

"Wait," Trish replies, surprised. "You got into a hot air balloon?"

I nod.

"Like, you actually went in the balloon, up in the sky?"

I nod again.

"Wow, I have to say, I didn't think you had the cojones," Trish laughs.

"Cojones?" I asked, confused.

"Oh, my gosh, Zoe. Balls!" Trish moves the camera view to her hips, awkwardly hunches over because her belly is protruding so far, and holds her hand between her legs like she's cupping a pair of… well you know. "I didn't think you had the balls!" she repeats.

Typical Trish. Ugh, and it also reminds me of the "blueberry muffins" I didn't get to eat.

"Well, it was a short ride," I reply. "As soon as Ethan pulled out the ring, I panicked and almost blacked out. It was so embarrassing."

I see Trish wave her hand in front of her phone. "Don't sweat it. As long as you made it back safely, that's all that matters. Plus, that can't be the most embarrassing thing that's happened in front of Ethan. I'm sure by now he knows all your silly quirks. What's that saying? 'You don't deserve me at my best if you can't handle me at my worst.'"

"Uh, yeah…" I reply hesitantly, but honestly, I've always tried my hardest to downplay all my quirks and negative attributes.

It's been excruciating hiding my obsession with *Twilight* this last year. After Ethan fell asleep out of boredom partway through the movie, I gave up on sharing that passion with him. Actually, I don't think Ethan would consider something like that a passion.

Anyway, my glasses have been stored away forever, and so has my side braid. Shaving once a week has turned into once a day. The last thing I want is for Ethan to discover I have a man-stache, and as long as I maintain it, he will never know.

"It makes me so happy you got what you wanted," Trish says. "I guess since you're engaged and all, I can tell you about Lee."

My eyes widen, excited to hear Lee's name out loud and to possibly hear some news about what's been going on in his life.

"Oh, Lee recently texted me," I mention.

"Aw. That's good to hear. I knew you guys would work things out. So, he must've already told you about his new girlfriend. I saw them eating yogurt together. Their public display of affection was off the charts! So much for 'get a room,' more like 'get some birth control.' I thought Lee was going to impregnate her on the yogurt shop table." Trish laughs.

I wish I could join in on her laughter, but my heart feels heavy, and I don't know why. Probably because Trish is breaking the news to me instead of Lee, or maybe it's the thought of Lee sitting with someone else, doing dirty things at *our* table. It would have been better if Lee told me first. After all, we tell each other everything, or at least, we used to.

Trish cringes, realizing my saddened expression. "I guess he didn't let you know?" she whispers.

I shake my head and swallow hard. "No," I reply, and abruptly change the disappointed look on my face. I smirk and put on a façade. "It's no big deal. I'm sure he would've told me eventually."

"Yeah… I think so too," Trish says.

"Of course," I reply, but neither of us seems one-hundred percent positive.

"Well, we don't need to talk about it. There's so much more I want to tell you, like, how Roy keeps clogging up our master bathroom toilet."

"Yeah… I rather not talk about—"

Trish clearly feels bad about bringing up Lee and doesn't drop the subject. "I think it's the old plumbing. Might be time to call a plumber because if it gets worse, our whole house will be flooded with Roy's crap. We will be drowning in Roy's—"

"Okay, Trish. I bet it can't be as bad as the plumbing at my old place."

"Oh, it is, definitely."

I sigh.

"All right, so, you don't want to hear about that. Then let's talk more about you coming to visit."

This subject is a better choice. "I do really want to visit."

"So, you should come and visit for a couple of weeks," Trish insists.

I think about all my duties here with Ethan. "I don't know… Ethan works a lot, and I need to take care of the house and make dinner."

Trish looks at me like I've gone mad. "If anyone knows how it is, I do. Trust me, but you also need to see your family. It's easier for you to visit me and the kids than me having to lug the children to see you."

"You have a valid point," I reply. "Maybe I can come and visit for a week."

"Good answer. Travis and Ashely will be so excited!" Trish walks over to the kids and tells them, "Hey, you guys, guess what? Auntie Zoe is coming to visit next week!"

"Trish!" I shout. "I said *maybe* and nothing about next week."

She ignores me, and to make matters worse, my niece and nephew are too busy bouncing up and down in excitement at the thought of me visiting them.

"Yay!" Trish yells along with them.

"I don't know if there will be any rooms available in the hotels nearby," I say.

"What are you talking about? You can stay with us. Don't waste your money on a hotel room."

The three of them are still celebrating. Ashley screams, "Auntie is coming!" and Travis chimes in and says, "Board games!"

I can't break their hearts, and I can't make up any more excuses. "Yup, Auntie will be there next week," I say. "I can't wait to see all of you."

If I'm being honest, Trish and the kids aren't the only ones I'm missing. I also can't wait to see Lee.

Chapter Five

Princess

Ethan and I sit at the dinner table after he returned from work.

"You did a phenomenal job on these stuffed shells," Ethan says as he ravenously eats his dinner.

I smile, happy Ethan is pleased with my hard work. "I'm glad you are enjoying it."

"But you usually only make these on special occasions."

"Oh, I know…"

Ethan pauses from stuffing his face. "I haven't forgotten anything, have I? Today's not your birthday, and we just celebrated our anniversary. I—"

"No, you haven't forgotten anything."

Okay, so I may have made Ethan's favorite dish for him because I wanted to butter him up before I announced I would be going to San Diego for a week.

"Phew!" Ethan responds. "Glad I'm in the clear."

"So, anyway!" I say. "I was thinking of visiting Trish and the kids."

"Oh," Ethan responds.

"Yeah, it's been a long time since we've seen each other."

"Has it?" he asks. "Well, I was planning on trying to visit for the holidays in a couple of months like I usually do. I'm pretty sure I can take more than just a week off."

"Um—" I stammer, thinking about how I already told Trish when I would visit. "Well, that would be nice to make another trip during the holidays, but Trish already told Travis and Ashely I would be going next week."

"Um, all right," Ethan replies, surprised. "I'm not quite sure I can get time off right now since my team and I have that big project we've been working on."

I look down at my plate, not wanting to tell him I am going without him. "Well…" I say, "I was thinking I can just go next week… by myself. I mean, if that's okay with you? I don't want you to feel stressed out having to take care of the house and meals. I know work has been a lot and everything."

Ethan places his hand on top of mine and smiles. It looks like a forced smile, but a smile, nonetheless. "No, don't worry about me. I will be fine."

"Okay," I reply and feel more at ease. "I would've asked you first, but Trish got all excited and jumped the gun on breaking the news to the kiddos."

"It's all right," Ethan says. "But if I starve to death, it's on your hands," he jokes.

"You got by just fine before you met me," I remind him.

"Yeah, but I don't think I can ever go back to TV dinners after being spoiled."

"I can always meal prep before I leave," I assure him.

Now I feel a bit like Cinderella after she got permission to go to the ball. If I want to go to San Diego, I need to get all my chores done. No problem. I can handle a week's worth of meal prep.

Chapter Six

Just a Dream

When Trish picked me up from the airport, she told me Roy had officially demolished their toilet the night before.

"Don't worry, though," she said. "I was able to find you a room at the Hyatt."

"The Hyatt?" I asked, shocked. "Did that cost you a fortune?"

"I won't deny it," Trish said. "But all of the other nearby hotels were full."

"I can't believe you did that," I replied.

"I know, but it's worth it. I can't have you staying in a sewer."

"I'm sure it's not that bad. I don't mind. I can call the hotel and cancel the reservation."

"It's too late for that. They require a day's notice, but seriously, all four of us are using the half bathroom downstairs. I wouldn't be surprised if Roy destroys that toilet as well. It's safer if you just stay away for the next day or two while the plumber gets it under control. So, that means, unfortunately, I'm going to be busy for the next couple of days until we can hang out."

"I can help," I mentioned.

"No, no," Trish replied. "I really am bummed. We wanted to spend as much time with you as we could. You will just have to extend your vacation."

I let out an awkward laugh. "Uh, yeah. I don't know about that. The clock will strike after seven days."

"Huh? What clock?" Trish asked.

"Nothing…" I replied.

"Well, we will see," Trish said, hopeful. "I hate to drop you off and run, but I was supposed to meet the plumber five minutes ago."

While Trish attends to her homeowner issues, I check into my hotel room. It's nice, but like every other hotel, it doesn't have any good TV shows or movies.

Just as I lie down on the bed and start watching a tutorial on my phone, I think about sending a text to Ethan to let him know I arrived safe and sound. I pull up my text messages, and I become sidetracked, looking at my most recent message from Lee. What kind of friend would I be if I didn't let Lee know I was in town, right?

All I want is for our relationship to go back to how it used to be, so I text Lee and say: *"Hey, Lee. Just letting you know, I'm in San Diego visiting for a little while. Let me know if you are free. I would really like to hang out with you."*

I pray hard for a response. Any response is better than no reply at all.

It worked. Lee replies: *"Not down for Twilight. How about fro-yo? I can meet you at our spot in twenty."*

I eagerly respond: *"I'm there!"*

I hop out of the hotel bed and rush to the bathroom to powder my nose and smooth out my hair. I've missed Lee more than anything. No one can replace him.

As I pull into the parking lot, I notice Lee has beaten me. Hopefully, he arrived early because he couldn't wait to see me. I excitedly exit the car and approach Lee, who is sitting at our usual table. I want to rush up to him. I want him to entangle me in a warm embrace, but I slowly walk toward him because he is on the phone with someone, laughing hysterically, so I stand a couple of feet away from the table and wave.

Lee finally notices I'm here and quickly says to the person on the other line, "Oh, hey, I have to go, but I will see you later tonight."

Lee hangs up the phone. He stands up and catches me off guard as he wraps his huge arms around me to give me a big bear hug. I didn't get a chance to open my arms to embrace Lee. I stand like a soldier whose arms are plastered by her sides and allow Lee to envelop my body in his warm embrace—the most comforting embrace I know.

"So, does this mean you forgive me?" I chuckle awkwardly.

Lee pulls away, which makes me regret speaking. I could've waited another minute before opening my mouth, and he would've held me that much longer.

"Yeah, my parents and Trish convinced me to stop being stubborn," Lee replies.

"Trish?" I ask, confused.

"Your sister can be really persuasive. Also, I'm deathly afraid of pregnant women. When they say to do something, you do it. I don't want to be the reason for Trish going into preterm labor."

I laugh, just like I used to at Lee's goofiness. "I know what you mean." Then I remember Trish telling me Lee had met someone. I wonder if that's who Lee was talking to on the phone when I arrived.

"Let's get in line before it starts wrapping even further around the building," Lee suggests.

"Good idea," I say, and as we walk to the back of the line, I can see Lee staring at me out of the corner of my eye. I look up at him. "Why are you giving me a death stare?"

"Death stare? I wouldn't consider it anything close to that."

"Okay, well, why are you looking at me like that?"

"I'm just trying to picture you like you used to be before you met Ethan."

"Why would you want to do that?" I ask, confused.

"You know why," Lee replies. I think he is trying to subtly say he still isn't fond of my "modern" look.

"Does it really matter?"

I'm not mad. I know Lee is being somewhat playful.

Lee shrugs. "I guess not. As long as you stay the same on the inside."

"I am," I state.

I mean, I think I am. I've become a better version of myself on the inside, like learning how to make a decent meal and being able to take care of a home. Just because I care about how I look on the outside doesn't make me a completely different person on the inside, or at least, I think.

"But if you decided not to obsess over lame vampire romance movies, I'd be okay with that," Lee adds.

I fake laugh and shoot Lee an evil glare. "Aren't you the comedian," I say and shove his shoulder. "I'm sure it's better than the movies your girlfriend makes you watch," I accidentally say out loud.

"How'd you know I have a girlfriend?" Lee asks, surprised.

"Uh… you know, word gets around." I wonder when Lee planned on mentioning he met someone.

"Who told you?" Lee asks and then answers his own question. "Oh yeah, that's right," he says. "I saw Trish when I was with Cynthia the other day."

Cynthia? Why does that name sound so familiar. I can't remember. Was it one of the girls at the reunion I didn't know all that well in high school? No, that's not it.

"Yeah, you're right," I admit, and then I remember who Cynthia is. "I thought hot chicks that look like K-pop stars weren't your type?"

Lee smooths his slicked-back hair, which is an uncomfortable response to my comment.

"I'm just joking around," I say. "So, what did you do? Illegally look up Cynthia's client information in the computer system at work?" I smirk.

Lee chuckles. "No, she scheduled a ton of sessions with me at the gym, and I also ran into her again while we were both getting yogurt shortly after you left."

"Oh…" I reply, disappointed my best friend has found someone to replace me on fro-yo dates, or every day for that matter.

"She's actually a nice person once you get to know her."

"Pretty modest, I bet," I say, taking a jab.

Lee doesn't respond to my comment, but he tries to subdue a smirk forming on his face.

I eagerly take a massive bite of my yogurt. "Holy cow!" I say as it melts in my mouth. I think my eyeballs rolled to the back of my brain for a second.

Lee laughs. "That good?"

I nod my head as I savor the fro-yo and continue to inhale the creamy goodness. "You don't know how much I've missed this."

"Not many yogurt places where you're living?" Lee asks.

"There's some, but Ethan bought me a frozen yogurt machine."

"Wow," Lee replies. "Fro-yo all day, every day, huh?"

"It's not as great as you make it sound. The machine doesn't make gourmet yogurt like what we are eating right now."

"Bummer," Lee responds. "Guess you will have to make more trips down here."

"I want to… I mean, I plan to. It's been hard being away from…" I hesitate. "Trish and the kids." I wanted to say "you," but it felt weird, so I didn't.

"I bet," Lee says.

"Anyway, tell me more about you and Cynthia."

"Not much to say."

"Really?" I look at Lee, annoyed. "Nothing at all?"

"Nope."

"You've been dating her for a year, and you really have nothing to say."

Lee shrugs, which is lame.

"Fine, whatever," I say.

"Why don't you tell me about Ethan?" Lee mentions.

I pretend to zip my lips. If he won't tell me about his girl, I'm not going to chit-chat about Ethan and my relationship.

"You don't even want to tell me what that's all about?" Lee asks as he points to the ring on my finger.

I quickly hide my hand underneath the table and cover the ring with my other hand. I had forgotten about that detail. I haven't thought about Ethan for the last hour—only when Lee brought him up.

"Why are you hiding it under the table?" Lee asks.

"Um, I—" I shake my head and chuckle uncomfortably, trying to think of a reason. "I'm not hiding it under the table."

"I think you are," Lee says, laughing.

I slouch and admit, "Fine. You're right." I slap my hand down on the table, so the ring is in plain view.

"That's a nice rock," Lee mentions.

"It is," I agree, staring at the massive diamond.

"You don't like it?" Lee asks, regarding the neutral expression on my face.

"No, it's not that," I reply.

"Not big enough for your taste?" Lee jokes.

I glare at Lee. "Yeah, that's it," I say sarcastically.

"Then what is it?"

Actually, Lee does present a good question. I want to say it's because Ethan does so much for me already, and he didn't need to splurge on me. I could explain I miss being away from Ethan when I look at the ring, but a more accurate answer would be, at the moment, it reminds me of how I lost my best friend for pursuing a relationship with Ethan.

"Nothing," I lie.

"Usually, recently engaged ladies like to show off their ring."

"I was going to flash it in your face, but I just forgot to mention it," I say defensively.

"How do you forget something like that?"

Another good question I don't know the answer to. Maybe it's because I didn't actually say "yes" to Ethan when he proposed, or it could possibly be the fact that Lee kissed me before I left—the most alluring kiss I've ever felt from anyone.

I imagine Lee's kiss was the same type of kiss someone would give another person who only has days to live. Or, you know, the exact kiss in one of those movies where the damsel is lying on the ground, taking in her last breath as her lover plants one last kiss on her lips before life leaves her body. Yeah, it was like one of those kisses, and one I will never forget.

"I don't know," I reply.

"You guys have a date picked out?" Lee asks.

"No, Ethan just proposed a few days ago."

"Hmm."

"What?" I ask, guarded.

"Oh, nothing," Lee says and continues to focus on his yogurt. I know he's still judging the fact that I "forgot" to mention I got engaged.

"Let's talk about something else," I suggest.

I'm slightly ashamed of myself for wanting to change the subject, but Lee is right, most girls flaunt their ring, and usually, you can't shut them up when they start talking about their future wedding.

Lee nods, accepting my request. "You staying at Trish's?"

"No, her bathroom flooded."

"That doesn't sound good."

"Yeah, I don't really know the extent of it, but it sounds pretty bad. She banned me from her house for the next two days until the plumber gets it under control, and the house gets cleaned up."

"So, where are you staying while you visit?"

"In a hotel," I mention. "The Hyatt."

"Wow, first-class, huh?"

"I know. Trish said she had trouble finding a cheaper place. Honestly, I would've been fine with a shanty motel."

"Would've reminded you more of your tiny studio?" Lee asks, laughing.

I shoot him a dirty look.

"I thought you booked the Hyatt because you've been living all luxuriously in Ethan's chateau." Lee makes some weird gesture with his hands, flickering in the air like a snooty person would do.

"What are you talking about?" I ask, offended. "Ethan owns a cabin… type of house."

"A cabin? Your dream really has come true then."

"What do you mean?"

"Like Bella and Edward's cabin. You know, the one they live in after they get married."

"That's a cottage, not a cabin," I say.

"Same thing."

"No, cabins are built with logs and have a completely different feel."

"Isn't that what's in the movie?"

"Uh, no."

"I'm positive it's a cabin," Lee says confidently.

"Anyway!" I shout, needing to change the subject again to break away from our debate. "There's not one good movie on the hotel TV. Well, not one that doesn't cost a ridiculous amount."

"I bet we can figure out some way to watch *Twilight*," Lee mentions. "We can chill tonight."

"You are voluntarily making plans with me to watch a movie you constantly complain about?"

"I just want to prove to you that it's a cabin and not a cottage."

I roll my eyes at Lee's unwillingness to admit he likes my choice of movies. "Wait… don't you have plans later? I thought I heard you tell whoever you were talking to on the phone that you would see her tonight?" I was positive Lee had plans with Cynthia.

"Shoot!" Lee yells and leans back into the chair, disappointed. He places his hand on his forehead. "I totally forgot."

"Jeez, Lee. How can you forget something like that?" I say, mocking him. "Most people wouldn't forget something like that—hot date with a K-pop star and all."

"Okay, you got me," he chuckles, but then he becomes serious. "Damn, sorry. I'm supposed to take Cynthia out to some restaurant on top of a hotel. She's been begging me to take her for weeks."

"It's cool," I say, hiding my true disappointment.

"But hey, I can hang out with you all day tomorrow. Cynthia has to work, and you said Trish will still be busy taking care of her plumbing issues."

"Yeah," I reply. "Tomorrow would be awesome. We can lounge by the pool. I heard a heatwave is supposed to sweep by."

"Sounds like a plan."

"And don't forget, you said you would watch *Twilight* with me," I remind Lee.

"Yeah, I know," Lee chuckles and stands up from the table. "I guess I better get going."

"Yeah… yeah, for sure," I say, wishing I could spend every second with Lee. "Don't want to miss out on your booty call," I joke, still trying to hide my true feelings.

"Yup, you know it."

Lee waves again as he pulls out of the parking lot. This is the first time we've left separately. I've always picked Lee up before our fro-yo dates. We've always left together, and even better, we usually watched a movie after at my place. I wasn't used to Lee walking away from me.

I lie in my hotel bed, bored and alone. The sun's still up, but my eyes slowly shut, and I drift away.

I see myself snuggled up with Lee on a couch—more specifically, the same couch Ethan and I share each night at his house. Lee has his arm wrapped around my shoulders, I lean my head on his chest, and we are both content. There's no dialogue in my dream, and for whatever reason, I only see our bodies from our chests and up. The only sound I hear is background noise coming from the TV. Goosebumps line my body from Lee repeatedly running his fingertips along the side of my upper arm. I look up and smile at him, Lee tenderly kisses me on my lips, and it's perfection, like stars aligning. It feels like everything is right in the world, or at least, my world, and that's good enough for me.

I try to hang onto my dream, but it becomes out of reach, and it completely fades away when I realize my phone is ringing. I swipe my finger along the screen and groggily answer the call.

"Hey! I'm glad you finally picked up. I was getting worried," Ethan says.

Huh? I look at my missed calls. Ethan tried calling me three times in a row.

"I'm sorry. I didn't mean to worry you. I meant to text you, but I, um—I got distracted," I explain.

"Distracted?"

"Uh, yeah. I was busy getting settled into the hotel, and then I ended up falling asleep."

"You're at a hotel? What happened to staying at Trish's?"

"She had some bad plumbing issues, so she found me a room at a nearby hotel."

"I see. Well, I'm glad you answered. So, what do you have planned for your stay?"

"Trish is preoccupied tomorrow, so I'll probably just hang out by the pool."

I bet you noticed I left out an important detail—Lee. Yeah, I know, I'm a terrible person.

"Did you bring a bathing suit?" Ethan asks seriously.

"I've made it a habit to always pack a bathing suit now," I laugh, trying to lighten the mood.

"Would I have something to do with it?" he asks sarcastically, and thankfully, Ethan isn't upset.

"Possibly," I joke.

"That's good to know," Ethan replies. "Wouldn't want anyone to get a free show."

"Like they would allow such a thing at a hotel in San Diego."

"Touché. So, you're just playing it solo for tonight and all tomorrow? That's not much fun. I know how much you miss your family."

"Yeah…" I lie.

I don't know where it's coming from, but guilt starts to present itself—guilt about Lee. Why am I lying to Ethan? There's nothing going on between us except that I believe we've mended our friendship. I should tell Ethan I'm hanging out with Lee tomorrow. All I've ever told Ethan, in the last year, is that Lee was upset I decided to move. Maybe I have changed. Maybe Lee's right. I never used to lie like this. I don't know if I can keep this up any longer.

Yeah, I think being more honest with Ethan is the right thing to do. I'd want to know if it were the other way around. If Ethan traveled and made plans to hang out with a girl, I think it would be respectful to tell me whether it was his longtime best friend or a stranger. A stranger would be worse anyway, right? Ethan won't be upset.

I clear my throat. "I mean, actually… Lee said he would keep me company tomorrow."

"Oh, Lee?" Ethan asks, surprised. "I thought he wasn't talking to you."

"He's finally forgiven me," I explain, trying not to sound too excited.

"That's good to hear," Ethan says and chuckles uncomfortably. "I have to admit, I was kind of relieved when you guys stopped talking to each other."

Ethan was relieved my best friend had been ignoring me? How horrible, but I know that's not how he meant it.

Actually, I don't understand why Ethan would say such a thing.

"Why were you relieved?" I ask, trying to give Ethan the benefit of the doubt before becoming upset.

It was really hard for me to be away from everyone I know for an entire year, let alone having my best friend act like I didn't exist.

"Uh, well…" Ethan mumbles. "I just always thought there might be something more than just friendship between you two."

"Are you crazy?" I ask.

"I don't think I'm crazy," Ethan says. "I walked in on you guys, and Lee was on top of you."

"I told you, nothing happened," I reply defensively.

"I know. I know. I didn't mean to bring up the past," Ethan says, retracting, but I'm annoyed he brought that back up, nonetheless. It's like he doesn't trust me or something.

"It's fine," I say, holding back my frustration.

"I don't want anything to come between us. I guess I'm just a little insecure when it comes to that topic."

"What topic?" I ask, but I have an idea of what Ethan is referring to, or I should say, *who* Ethan is referring to. "You mean you feel unsure when it comes to Lee?"

"Yeah," Ethan answers.

"Seriously?" I ask, shocked.

Ethan insecure? Like I mentioned, Ethan is swoony in every way. He's a ten out of ten—a solid, hot ten with an amazing job! It makes no sense that Ethan would be insecure.

"You obviously don't see the way he looks at you."

"What are you talking about, Ethan?" I ask, still annoyed.

"Lee doesn't look at you like he just wants to be friends."

"You aren't making any sense."

"Oh, come on, Zoe!" Now Ethan is becoming just as frustrated as I am. "Lee wants you, and I know he does. He doesn't want to just be your friend. I'm a guy, so take it from me. I know how we operate. Until we tie the knot, I don't see him throwing in the towel."

"You don't need to worry," I assure Ethan. "Nothing is going on between Lee and me. I, um—" I stutter, trying to push the memory of Lee's kiss away from my thoughts. Once that memory is dismissed, I say firmly, "Whether you are right or wrong, you don't have anything to worry about. You can trust me. I only think of Lee as a friend. Remember, I've spent the last year with you, not Lee."

Ethan doesn't respond for a while like he's thinking things over.

"You know, I can't wait to set a date for the wedding," I add, attempting to put Ethan at ease.

"Oh, yeah?" Ethan asks.

"Yeah," I reply. "We should set it in stone when I get back home."

"I can't wait. That's a great idea," Ethan says happily.

"Did you already eat your pasta?" I ask.

"Just about to, but it's not the same without you here. I've enjoyed your company since you moved in. It's lonely tonight."

"Aw, it's hard to be away from you too," I say, but honestly, I'm okay. I didn't know Ethan was so needy. I didn't know someone could fall for me so hard. Not in a million years did I actually think I could have a man wrapped around my finger. "Well, I better let you get something in your belly after a hard day's work."

"I'll call you tomorrow night," Ethan says.

"I will wait for your call," I assure him before hanging up.

After I let Ethan go, I realize I haven't entirely gotten rid of the guilt. It's still lingering. I'm pretty sure it's multiplying as I think about what I hadn't told Ethan. The guilt spreads while I think back to my most recent dream.

Was it wrong that I had an intimate dream with a different person other than my fiancé? It's not like I can control what enters my brain while I'm asleep. Although I think I remember reading something about how dreams show you your subconscious thoughts. If that were true, then that means I do have feelings for Lee. Not just friendly feelings, but like, real lovey-dovey feelings, which means I just lied to Ethan, but it was *just a dream*, and those studies about dreams aren't definite. It didn't really happen. I didn't actually have those feelings while snuggled up with Lee. It's not like it was real.

Like I said… it was just a dream.

Chapter Seven

Stay

Lee and I find a pair of lounge chairs by the pool.

"You don't know how excited I am that we get to spend *all day* together," I tell Lee, removing my shirt and shorts, revealing my bikini. "You can stay and eat dinner with me, right?"

I'd prefer to be by myself and bored to death in a hotel room as little as possible.

"Me too," Lee replies. "Yeah, but I promised Cynthia I would swing by her place for a little after she gets off work. I might have to eat and run, and we should probably watch *Twilight* during dinner just to be safe. Oh, that's if you were planning on ordering room service? If not, I think I might have to take a rain check on the movie."

I really hate having to share Lee. "Okay," I say, trying not to sound bummed out. "We can order in."

I sit down on the chair but pause from lying down as Lee pulls his shirt over his head, showcasing his perfect body. I try not to stare, but my eyes are glued to his chiseled torso.

"So awesome to have a heatwave in the middle of autumn," Lee says.

"Uh... huh," I respond, still transfixed on Lee's gorgeous body.

I've always known Lee had the perfect physique. I mean, he is a physical trainer after all and works out all the time. This is nothing new to me, but for some reason, I think I'm admiring him in a completely different way. Someone might need to come wipe the drool off the corner of my mouth.

Lee squeezes a dollop of sunscreen onto the palm of his hand, and I can feel my heart start to race as I witness him run his hands over each of his defined muscles. My skin becomes dewed with sweat watching Lee finish up.

"You want some?" Lee asks, trying to hand me the bottle of sunscreen.

I don't realize Lee is addressing me.

"Do... *you* want some sunscreen?" he repeats himself.

"Oh, uh, yeah." I chuckle. "I'd better. We both know how easily I burn."

I quickly grab the sunscreen and transition my eyes to a mom and dad playing with their toddler in the pool. The last thing I want is for Lee to realize I'm checking him out. That would be so awkward.

"I know," says Lee in a mocking tone. "I remember that one time we went to the fair, and you refused. What was your excuse?"

"Please, don't remind me."

"Oh yeah, now it's coming back to me. You wanted to try to get a tan so you could look like one of those girls in your magazines you used to obsess over."

"Yup…" I reply, annoyed thinking about the memory.

Lee continues, "You had me rub aloe on your back for a week straight."

"How could I forget?" I grumble.

"You should've opted for some sunscreen, then our classmates wouldn't have had a reason to compare you to a dirty tampon."

"Wow, you really know how to continue on with a sore subject. You know, those kids were so cruel," I mention, angrily throwing the bottle of sunscreen on the ground. "So many other things are red—cherries, watermelon… roses!" I lie down and cross my arms, fuming.

"Lighten up, Zoe," Lee laughs. "It was almost fifteen years ago. But you know, just to steer safely away from more name-calling, maybe I ought to put some on your back for you."

"I'm okay," I reply. "The sun's not hitting my back anyway."

"For now, until we go into the pool."

I ignore Lee. Plus, I don't want to go into the pool and ruin my hair and makeup.

"Jeez, Zoe, stop being stubborn, and let me get your back."

"You didn't put any on yours," I argue.

"Well, you didn't let me finish," Lee says. "I was going to have you put some on me too."

"Fine," I say, giving in and hold out my hand, instructing Lee to place the sunscreen in my palm.

Lee picks up the bottle but doesn't hand it to me. "Uh-uh," he says. "You first."

I frustratedly sit up. "Ugh, whatever," I say in a snooty voice.

Lee doesn't squirt the sunscreen onto his palm. Instead, he spurts it all over my back and laughs.

"Lee!" I yell.

"What?"

"That's not how you are supposed to do it."

"How do you know? Are you a professional cabana girl?"

"What are you talking about? That doesn't even make any sense. Cabana girls don't provide sunscreen service."

"Depends on where you're at."

"Okay, sure," I reply. "So, does this mean you are my cabana boy?"

"I'll be whatever you want me to be," Lee says sarcastically, or I think he's being sarcastic.

I look over my shoulder to see Lee smirking, and rather than just applying the sunscreen to my back, I feel his fingers sliding along the sides of my stomach. I breathe in deeply, enjoying his touch. Lee pulls my hair to the side of my shoulder, and as he runs his hand on the back of my neck, I can't help but compare the feelings I'm encountering right this moment to the ones I've had with Ethan in the bedroom. Lee is taking his time, and I start to freak out. I shouldn't be thinking about Lee in that kind of light.

"Okay!" I abruptly say, "That's nice. I—I mean, good enough. It's good enough. Your turn."

"What? I wasn't doing a good job?" Lee asks.

"You did, um, a super-duper job. Thanks," I say uncomfortably. "Sit down, and I'll do yours." I grab the bottle from his hand a little too aggressively.

Luckily, Lee doesn't announce I'm acting a little off. He sits down beside me and turns his back to me.

As I'm about to place my hand onto Lee's body, I freeze. Do I want to touch him like he touched me? I should've brought the spray kind like I usually do. It would've made things a lot less confusing and awkward.

"Everything okay back there?" Lee asks, waiting.

"Oh, um. Yeah," I reply and quickly smear it onto his back like an overly excited toddler fingerpainting and lie back down.

"Uh, all right. Not sure you got all the spots," Lee says, but thankfully doesn't protest any further.

"Anyway," I say, closing my eyes, trying to forget about how I just acted like a weirdo. "I really needed this."

Lee looks over at me and smiles. "I know, it's been too long."

"It was terrible not talking to you for so long."

"I shouldn't have ignored you like I did," Lee admits.

"I understand," I say. "I'd be mad if you left me, like... if it was the other way around."

"But you would never do that to me. You'd never ghost me," Lee replies.

"You always give me too much credit."

"Never," Lee responds. "Plus, it's not like you feel the same way I feel about you."

"You mean felt—felt about me."

"Uh... yeah," Lee says. "*Sure*, that's what I meant."

Okay, now I'm really confused. Did Lee mean to say it how I thought he meant it? I figured Lee got over me, and that's why he moved on to Cynthia. There's no way Lee can still have those kinds of feelings for me. Or maybe the "feelings" Lee was referring to were feelings of friendship, like, he has *stronger* friendship feelings toward me. Yeah, that has to be it.

"Um, so, anyway," I say, changing the subject—a subject that won't lead me down a road to feelings of guilt. One that won't make me ponder Lee's and my relationship. "What do you and Cynthia have planned for tonight?"

"Massage."

"What?" I ask, confused.

"Cynthia requires a massage every night before bed."

"That's… cool," I reply, not fully understanding.

"And a foot massage."

"Hold up. So, are you saying you go over to Cynthia's every night to give her a massage before she goes to bed?"

"Uh-huh," Lee says nonchalantly.

"Wow… you sure are committed."

"I know. If there were ever a 'Best Boyfriend' award, I would win that sucker, or at least be nominated."

"Uh, yeah. Agreed." We chuckle together, but my mind wanders back to the moment Lee's hands were on my body. I can see why Cynthia would want Lee to rub her down on a nightly basis.

"But I'm sure Ethan does a lot for you too," Lee says.

I nod and try to think of the things he does for me. "He takes good care of me."

"What are some of the things he does for you? I want to make sure he's treating you right," Lee says in a joking tone.

"I, um… well, he pays all the bills, and he, uh… took me on a nice trip to Napa recently."

"So, you got yourself a sugar-daddy," Lee says.

"That's not what I said at all."

"That's what I heard," Lee counters.

"Well, you heard wrong."

Then I begin to wonder if Ethan would give me a massage every night if I asked him. His documentaries are really important to him, and he'd probably fall asleep in the middle of rubbing my back like he does in the middle of watching vampire romances.

"Yeah, I know… you are going to tell me to shut it, and I'm always wrong," Lee says and then abruptly hops up. "Let's get into the pool now. It's hot, hot, hot."

I shake my head. "Go by yourself. I'm mad at you for calling me a gold-digger."

Lee throws his hands into the air. "Now you are putting words into my mouth."

I'm not really all that mad. I'm just slightly agitated Lee subtly called me a gold-digger. I fold my arms across my chest, exaggerating my anger.

"You said it," I say firmly, sticking my nose in the air. "And I don't want to mess up my hair and—"

"That's it!" Lee screams and scoops me off the chair.

"No, no!" I shout while kicking my feet. "You wouldn't dare!"

"You asked for it!"

"No, stop! I'll get in!" I shout, pleading. "Just don't get my face wet. I didn't put the right kind of makeup on!"

Lee walks over to the edge of the pool. "Oh, it's too late for that," he says playfully and gives a good swing before throwing me into the water.

I quickly stand up in the pool, gasping for air, and angrily yell, "Lee! Why would you do that?" I wipe my fingers along the bottom of my eyes in an attempt to fix my runny mascara. "Now I look like the Joker from *Batman.*"

Lee ignores me, takes a couple of running steps, and does a cannonball into the pool. I notice the family beside us laughing as the calm water turns to small waves.

Lee pops up from under the water. "You look gorgeous. Plus, I haven't seen your wavy hair in over a year."

I focus on combing through my tangled hair with my fingers.

"Stop thinking about your hair and makeup for once!" Lee shouts and places his hands on my sides, and then he throws me into the air like parents do with their kids. I find myself completely submerged under the water again.

I come up for air a second time, but this time with a vengeance. "Oh, you're going down!" I yell.

"Really?" Lee asks, laughing. "Bring it."

I walk toward him, jump as high as I can into the air, slam my hands onto his upper chest, and try to submerge Lee.

"Weak..." Lee jokes, wrapping his arms around me as my body slides against his from a failed dunking attempt.

"You are the worst," I scream and try to give him a good slap again, but I realize Lee has trapped me in his famous bear hold.

"Am I?" Lee asks as our eyes meet.

"Yeah... I hate you," I joke, but as I continue to look at Lee, I become comforted.

I forget about my smudged makeup and natural hair. I don't think about Lee passing judgment on me. In Lee's arms, I feel perfect. In his embrace, I am loved, and if Lee can love me for what I look like under layers of makeup, why can't I love myself too?

Lee softly replies, "All right, but here's the thing... I don't hate you, Zoe."

I notice something different about Lee. He's looking at me in a strange way. Then I remember what Ethan said. Ethan mentioned he thought Lee looked at me like he wanted me. Could Lee be telling me something with his eyes? Does Lee *want* me?

"I... know," I whisper, falling deeper into Lee's gaze. "I could never really hate you. That's just what I always say."

I realize I have placed my hand on Lee's cheek. I don't recall Lee letting my arms release from my sides, but somehow, they are free. I look at where my hand had landed, and my eyes make their way to Lee's lips. Lee's lips look different as well—lips I desire. Lips that would fit perfectly against mine, so I bring mine closer to his while placing a second hand on the other side of his face. The sun hits the diamond on my finger, reminding me what we are doing is wrong. I quickly push myself away.

"Just kidding," I say, awkwardly as I float in the water, away from Lee's reach. "I really do hate you," I try to joke.

Lee looks like Cassie had just been run over by a semi-truck, and there's no hope left of survival.

"Hey, why don't we go wash up and get dinner?" I suggest. "Cynthia will be expecting you pretty soon."

Lee nods, defeated and hops out of the pool first. Lee's head hangs low as we quietly walk back to my hotel room. I feel horrible, and I don't want Lee to ignore me for another year, or worse, forever.

The silence is killing me and making me feel uncomfortable. I slide the hotel key into the reader, and the door breaks the silence, awkwardly squeaking open.

I head toward the bathroom and turn on the shower so the water will heat up. "You want to shower first, or should I?" I ask Lee as I shut the shower door.

He doesn't respond. So, I walk out of the bathroom thinking he hadn't heard me. Lee is seated on the edge of the bed, and I witness a lonely tear stream down his cheek.

I rush over to him. "What's wrong?" I ask.

Lee shakes his head and doesn't reply.

"Hey, it's okay," I say, unsure how to respond, seeing as I'm most likely the reason for Lee becoming upset.

Lee wipes away the tear and looks up at me, but now I think he might be angry. "It's not okay, Zoe!" Lee slams his fist onto the bed.

"What do you mean?" I ask, confused.

"This!" Lee shouts. "Us!"

"I'm sorry, um, about what happened in the pool. I—I hope I didn't cross the line. The last thing I want is to upset Cynthia or—"

"See!" Lee interrupts. "That's just it!" Lee stands up with flames in his eyes and begins to pace back and forth. "I wanted to kiss you in the pool—I wanted *you* to kiss me," Lee explains passionately. "It was torture being away from you an entire year. I lost my mind when you left me. I thought if I was able to cut ties with you, I would be fine. I thought if I started dating someone, I could get you out of my head, but it was useless."

Lee has smoothed back his hair about five times in a minute and is now scrunching his head between his hands. I don't want him to be upset. I don't want to lose my best friend.

"I'm sorry. I mean, I get what you are saying."

"No, you don't, Zoe," Lee growls. "You don't understand anything!"

"Um… so what don't I understand exactly?" I ask quietly.

Now Lee is pointing his finger at random things around the room. "You don't understand that you left me for Ethan. You don't understand that you had to change yourself to get some guy's attention."

"Please, Lee… I don't want to fight."

But he continues, "You don't understand. I can treat you better than any man. You don't get it at all!" He turns and points to me and then himself. "*We* are meant to be together."

"I—I… don't know what to say. I'm, uh… sorry for hurting you. Please, I don't want you to be mad at me again."

Lee inhales deeply and walks toward me, calmer. "I'm sorry," he says. "I didn't mean to make it seem like I'm upset at you." Lee gently places his hands on the sides of my shoulders and looks down at me. "I'm actually upset at myself for not making a move sooner. I had over a decade to tell you how I felt about you."

I stare at Lee in shock. He has the same look in his eyes—the same look he had in the pool earlier. The same look that's telling me Lee desires me.

"Zoe, what you don't understand is, I can't *just* be friends with you. I can't turn it off. I wish I told you I loved you sooner before you ran into Ethan again. I'd give anything to be the one to decide whether I love you or not, but I can't. My feelings for you won't go away, no matter how hard I try. I want nothing more in the world than for you to let me love you."

My heart is knocking hard against my chest as I take in every word Lee says. "You mean… you *love me… love me*?"

"Yes, Zoe. I love you, love you. How many ways do I need to tell you before you get it through that thick skull of yours?" Lee chuckles. "I love you as in, I never want to let you go. As in you are the only one for me."

"Oh, okay…" I reply. The worst possible response I could've come up with. I know, but can you blame me? I'm still in shock.

"Just, okay?" Lee asks. "You know, I'm pretty sure you love me too. You just won't admit it for whatever reason."

Is Lee right? Do I love him more than just a friend? Could we ever be something more?

Lee wraps his arms around me again. "I would never forgive myself for not trying one last time to make you realize we are meant for each other," Lee whispers into my ear. "God made you for me."

My legs feel tingly like I'm standing on a mountain top, thousands of feet in the sky. Lee places his lips on mine, but instead of pulling away, I kiss him back, and the sensation in my limbs spreads deep within my bones. An undeniable craving for Lee courses through my veins, and serenity clouds my mind.

Lee removes my shirt, and I take a step away from him.

"I'm sorry," Lee says, shaking his head. "I don't know what came over me. I've just waited so long for you to realize you feel the same way about me. I probably should just leave now—we can forget this ever happened." Lee starts gathering his belongings. "I shouldn't have taken off your—"

"No," I reply. I don't want Lee to leave.

Lee pauses and faces me.

I walk closer to him and run my hand through his hair. "Stay. Stay with me," I whisper.

Lee drops everything he has in his hands and forcefully pulls my body against his. Pins and needles make their comeback as Lee kisses my lips, and I have never wanted anyone as bad as I want Lee right this moment.

Lee picks me up, and I wrap my legs around him. He walks us toward the shower and gently places me in it. The sensations developing on my inner thighs are a hundred degrees hotter than the water pouring down on my body—anticipating what's to come.

Well, turns out it was a quick shower because getting down and dirty in a bathroom isn't anything like how it is in the movies. Lee about fell over and split his head, and the water from the showerhead kept beading off Lee and spraying me in the face. If I'm being honest, it's awkward and difficult.

So, eventually, Lee made the executive decision to throw me down onto the hotel bed. His kisses wander along my body, still wet from our shower. His hands continue to journey to places they've never been before, and Lee's lips find a new meaning in my dictionary as they linger in all the right spots. Every second I'm entangled with Lee is better than a thousand of my fantasies combined.

And as you can probably guess, that night, we skipped dinner entirely and went straight to dessert. Cynthia didn't get her nightly massage, and Ethan didn't get the late-night chat I promised him, but I've never had a night where things felt so right.

Chapter Eight

The Morning After

When I awoke, I reached over for Lee but noticed the bed was empty beside me. All I found was a note on the pillow, or better yet, a poem.

Last night was the best night ever,
I wanted to stay in bed with you forever,
But I know you're starving from skipping dinner last night,
So, as you can probably guess, I went to grab us a quick bite.

I don't know how I could've been so dumb. I think back to the sweet Christmas present Lee gave me and realize Lee has been subtly trying to tell me his true feelings all along. What did that poem say exactly? Actually, I think I still have it in my purse. I shuffle through my bag, pulling out items I don't necessarily *need* to be lugging around in my purse. You know, like, half-year-old receipts and a smushed protein bar. You never know when you might need a snack. Anyway, what do you know… the poem is shoved all the way at the bottom of my junky bag.

The picture of Edward Cullen smiles back at me before I open the semi-crumpled card. I reread Lee's confession. Yeah, I really don't know how I could've been so oblivious to Lee's feelings. Now, I see my Christmas present was more than just a physical gift, and I regret not taking better care of it. I was too distracted by the attention I was receiving from Ethan while Lee was trying to pour his heart out to me.

I shove all the crap back into my purse, but not the card. I don't want it to disappear at the bottom of the bag again, and not my phone because— "Shit!" I say aloud, noticing the notifications on the screen. I quickly phone Ethan, hoping he's not mad at me for ignoring his phone calls last night.

"Thank God," Ethan says, answering his phone.

"I'm so, so, sorry," I say.

"I was thinking of flying to San Diego if I didn't hear back from you soon!" Ethan says firmly.

I hope he's joking.

"What happened?" Ethan asks. "I thought you were going to wait by the phone."

"I—um," I stammer. I really should've thought of an excuse before making my phone call. "I fell asleep again."

"Oh… all right. Trip must really be taking a toll on you."

I continue to lie, "You know, when there's nothing to do, you just fall asleep watching a boring TV show."

"How long did Lee stay? Did you guys go out to dinner?" Ethan asks.

"Uh, he didn't stay long."

You'd think I didn't mind lying at the rate I'm going, but honestly, I really do hate lying to people. Especially people I care about. I've convinced myself I just need time to think everything over, and it will all be fine.

"That's good to hear, but hey, I actually can't talk long. I was in the middle of a meeting. I just wanted to make sure everything was okay. Please pick up when I call you tonight, all right?"

"I promise," I tell Ethan and praise God for Ethan's meeting.

"I love you more than anything," he says.

"I love you too," I say quietly because I do love Ethan.

I love Ethan but also love Lee, and I never thought in a million years that my heart would be torn between two people.

Shortly after, Lee returns with a paper plate wrapped in foil. "Guess what I picked up for you?" he asks me excitedly and places the plate on the table.

I walk over, intrigued. "Do I make my guess after I take the foil off?" I joke.

"That would be cheating," Lee laughs.

"You're right. Wouldn't want to ruin the fun," I reply and breathe in the umami aroma in the air.

"Chinese food?" I ask.

"More specific," Lee says.

"Your *mom's* Chinese food?"

"Okay, close enough," Lee replies and unveils my plate of food.

"Yay!" I shout and clap my hands. "Pork buns! My favorite!"

"I asked my mom to make them especially for you."

I give Lee a hug, thanking him for his thoughtful gesture. "You are so awesome." I take a heaping bite, and my eyes roll to the back of my head. "So, good!"

"I thought you'd like that."

"You know me too well."

Lee leans in and kisses me, but I don't kiss him back.

"What's the matter?" Lee asks, confused.

"Nothing," I lie, but I'm thinking about Ethan since I just got off the phone with him. "Was Cynthia upset you bailed on her last night?"

"Yeah, but she was even more upset when I swung by her house before going to pick up the buns at my mom's."

"You went by Cynthia's house this morning?"

"Well, I wanted to break up with her as soon as possible. That sounds bad, but you know what I mean… considering what happened last night."

I nod, feeling uncomfortable Lee had called it off with Cynthia.

"So, have you called Ethan yet, or do you still need to call him?"

"I called him while you were gone, but he couldn't talk for long," I explain.

"You mean he didn't want to get into the details about you leaving him?"

"Um… not exactly."

"He'd rather talk about it in person?"

I shake my head. "No."

Then Lee realizes what I've been trying to hint at as he looks at the ring still on my finger. "You didn't tell him about last night, did you?"

I cringe and shake my head again, ashamed.

"But you are going to, right?" Lee asks, hopeful.

"I… don't know," I reply.

"Are you kidding me?" Lee says angrily.

"I just need some time to think about it," I say pleadingly.

"What's there to think about, Zoe?" Lee fumes. "Don't go back to denying everything. Don't do this."

"I'm not," I try to say confidently.

"Yes, you are!" Lee shouts. "You still can't admit that you want to be with me. I thought after last night we'd be together."

I sit down on the bed and place my hands over my eyes, wanting this predicament to solve itself.

"I—I do have feelings for you, but I still have feelings for Ethan too. I feel terrible for cheating on him. He's been nothing but loyal. Ethan doesn't deserve what I've done to him."

"Make your decision now," Lee demands. "Now, or I'm leaving for good."

I look up at Lee in disbelief. "Lee, don't say that," I reply softly.

"I'm serious, Zoe. I'm done playing games."

"I just need a minute to think," I say, starting to panic.

I don't want to lose Lee again, but I also don't want to hurt Ethan. Both have done so much for me, and though it's selfish, I want both of them in my life.

"Fine. Take all the time you need," Lee says as he heads toward the door.

I abruptly stand up and reach my arm out for him, and for a split second, I have hope when Lee pauses and slowly walks back toward me. His eyes have filled with tears, and Lee places a single hand on my cheek. He speaks in a calm voice, "Ethan doesn't know you like I know you, and he will never be able to love you like I would."

Lee kisses me gently on my forehead, leaving me frozen and speechless before he walks out the door. I force my body to react and lurch toward him, but my hand slides down the door as it shuts. I'm too late.

"Lee!" I yell, knowing my efforts are pointless. "Don't go!" I scream but know Lee is long gone.

My chest tightens, and tears flood my eyes. I crumble to the ground like an abandoned child left in the cold—alone and afraid of what's to come.

Chapter Nine

Make up or Break up

The next morning, I'm interrupted by loud banging on my hotel door. "Open up!" I hear someone scream.

I roll myself out of bed and quickly braid my unruly hair. "One minute!" I shout.

"I know you're in there, Zoe!"

"Trish?" I say to myself as I give up on looking somewhat presentable and open the door.

Trish rushes in with a huge beach bag on her shoulder. She's holding Ashley, and Travis is beside her.

"You look like you've spent the night in Hell," Trish says, referring to the bags under my eyes from not sleeping all night and my bright red eyeballs from crying for the last twenty hours.

"Thanks," I grumble.

Travis hugs me tightly. "We've missed you, Auntie."

"Aw," I say and bend over to Travis' level. "I missed you too, buddy."

"The kids wanted to see you," Trish says. "I tried to call you, like, fifty times this morning."

"I had a rough night," I reply.

"Yeah, I can see that."

I plop back into bed and place the pillow over my face. "Just kill me now," I say.

"I can't do that," Trish says.

"You can," I murmur through the pillow. "Just hold this pillow over my face and count to one-hundred. I've seen it done in movies a thousand times."

"I could never do that," Trish says, yanking the pillow away from me. "Not while the kids are present," she jokes.

Travis starts jumping on the bed and singing the song about monkeys bumping their heads. Ashley is opening drawers and trying to find items to entertain herself.

"So, should we talk about what's going on here and let the kids terrorize the hotel room, or should we go to the park and let the monsters run around there?"

"Park," I answer. "Wait. I thought you were going to say the beach."

"Oh, because I have my oversized beach bag?"

"Well, yeah," I reply.

"I always carry this bag when we go places."

"You do?"

"Okay, it's a new addition, but yes, because I realized it's good for holding my water bottle."

Trish pulls out a gigantic jug that matches her ridiculously large bag. The bottle is filled with some kind of fruit juice. Maybe?

"And that's not cranberry juice in it, or at least that's what I'm telling myself," Trish says proudly.

"What did you bring?" I ask, confused.

"It's a mocktail. I looked up a recipe online. It's supposed to taste close to an alcoholic drink."

"Wow, why didn't you just get a flask?"

Trish scoffs and shakes her head. "People don't make sixty-four-ounce flasks. Seriously, Zoe, don't you know these things?"

"Guess not…" I reply, too drained to think of a comeback.

"I will share with you, but you have to act like it's the real thing," Trish demands.

"Well, I'm not a big fan of cranberry juice, as you know."

"There's, like, a splash of cran juice in it. Just humor me. I need this."

"Well, I will say, I could use a drink… or two," I reply, playing along.

"Now you're talking!" Trish shouts excitedly.

We walk to the park that's just around the corner from my hotel and find a bench in front of the jungle gym. The kids run around, entertaining themselves, and Trish doesn't hesitate to pull out the juice.

"So, were you planning on staying for dinner tonight?" I ask Trish as she takes a heaping gulp.

She wipes her moist lips on her wrist and hands me the bottle. I take a sip.

"Hey!" I say, surprised. "This isn't bad for a mocktail. It does taste like it has real—"

"Ah!" Trish shouts, interrupting me while holding up a finger. "Remember, it *is* the real thing!"

"Oops. My bad." I take another drink. "Wow, this cocktail is so strong! So boozy!"

Trish looks pleased with my performance and nods. "I know, it's the best drink I've ever had," she says.

"I agree," I reply, trying my best not to laugh.

"Anyway, I told Roy he is going to have to fend for himself tonight," Trish explains. "The kids will be tuckered out after running around, so I'm inviting myself over and staying the night. After all, I did pay for the hotel room with my stripper money."

"You mean your money from cleaning your elderly neighbor's house once a month?"

I knew Trish cleaned Ms. Hollister's house, but only after the kids and Roy had fallen asleep. For whatever reason, she wanted to keep it a secret from Roy. I don't think he wanted Trish to work. He likes being the "man of the house" or something like that.

Anyway, Trish had a pretty good amount saved up from her secret night job. She kept it in a coffee can under the kitchen sink, where she also kept the cleaning supplies. It was a safe bet Roy wouldn't look there.

"No way," I said, shocked. "*You* told Roy you weren't going to cater to him tonight?"

"Mhmm," Trish answers.

"*You,* the perfect homemaker?"

Trish rolls her eyes. "Yes. I finally put my foot down. Well, a little. I told Roy I need a break every now and then. It doesn't have to be once a week or even once a month, but I deserve some 'me time' once in a while."

"Wow, I am really proud of you," I reply.

"Thanks," Trish says happily. "It was hard, but I did it, and if you never said anything, I probably wouldn't have done it."

"Really?" I ask, surprised.

"Yes, when you got upset about how much I did for the family and how little Roy helped out, I started to think about my happiness and what I want. Then after that talk, we had about my acting career and whatnot, I thought about all the sacrifices I've made and thought about how Roy could make some too. Plus, I know marriages shouldn't be one-sided, and it should be a team effort. I just saw how Mom was when Dad left her, and I guess I thought that's what a wife was supposed to do. I wasn't willing to admit it before now."

"I understand," I tell Trish. "And I don't blame you, I mean, if we are admitting our wrongs… I've been going down the same path with Ethan."

"You feel like a stay-at-home slave?" Trish asks and then chuckles.

"Kind of…"

"You can say it."

"Okay, yeah. Not only that, all the physical upkeep is exhausting," I reply. "But Ethan's really great. I don't want to rag on him."

"I see," Trish says. "So, you and Ethan are good?"

I think for a moment. Ethan still doesn't know about what happened between Lee and me, so until then, we are fine. "Yeah, we're good."

"So, if you weren't crying over Ethan last night, then you must've been bawling over Lee?"

"How did you guess?" I ask, surprised Trish predicted what had been eating me up inside.

"Did you guys finally have your first kiss?" Trish looks intently at me, trying to guess my answer. I cringe, thinking about how we did more than just kiss. Trish grabs the bottle from my hand, slowly raises it to her mouth, and squints at me like she's trying to read my mind. Before she takes another drink, she realizes what really happened between Lee and me. "Oh, my God! You guys did *it!* You did the nasty."

I shut my eyes for a second and sigh. There's no hiding anything from my sister. "Yup," I admit.

"I knew it. *I knew it!* That look on your face is a dead giveaway!"

"I can't believe you could tell from just my expression," I reply, becoming frustrated.

"Honestly, Zoe, you are the worst at reading people. I should give you some pointers. I mean, you couldn't even tell Lee wanted you from day one. I seriously think you were the only one who couldn't figure it out."

"But I did eventually figure it out," I reply, annoyed.

Trish laughs. "Yup, you sure did," she says sarcastically. Trish takes a few more gulps of mocktail. "Anyway, spill," she demands.

"It's a long story," I reply, not wanting to relive my argument with Lee.

Trish spreads her hand through the air like she's surveying the landscape. "Um, I think we've got some time, Zoe."

"Yeah, okay. Well, it was the best night I've ever had."

Trish leans back onto the bench and gasps. "You mean the best SEX you've ever had?" she shouts.

"Shh!" I look around, making sure people are at a distance.

Trish leans toward me and thankfully talks softer. "How long?"

My eyes widen at my sister's blunt question.

She stares at me, disappointed I haven't given her any details yet. "Whatever. Be selfish and don't tell me."

"Most people don't share those details, even with their sister," I scoff.

"You don't know what it's like. I would've never guessed years of marriage, and two and a half babies later would result in lack of excitement in the bedroom."

"Please, Trish, let's not—"

"Nowadays, Roy just lies there like a limp fish. I might as well be making love to a lifeless body. I could buy one of those dolls and call it a day."

"No more!" I shout.

"Whatever. All I'm saying is Lee's body is hot, so I bet last night was *hot*," Trish adds. "Honestly, I'm surprised it didn't happen years ago. You guys were always two peas in a pod."

We were, weren't we? We went together like apples and peanut butter, or chips and guacamole—the perfect pair.

Trish continues, "I don't know how it is with Ethan, but I can tell you this much. I would give anything to have a deeper connection with Roy. We barely speak more than a couple of sentences to each other when he gets home from work. Most of my conversating throughout the day is reliant on the kiddos, and most of the time, they're in school, so if I'm being honest, a lot of the time, I talk to myself."

"How sad," I laugh.

"You laugh now, but just you wait," Trish replies.

"I don't understand, Trish," I say softly. "If you aren't happy, why don't you just get out?"

Trish looks at her children joyfully playing on the slide together. "I could never break up my family. It would feel wrong." My sister looks down at her bottle, which is almost empty. "You know how it felt only having one parent. The last thing I want to do to Travis and Ashley is make them experience what we went through."

"That's not the same," I say. "We never saw Dad because he abandoned us. He didn't want anything to do with us. We both know, even though Roy would rather sip on a beer than hang out with the kiddos, he still loves them. He'd still want to be a part of their lives."

"You're right," Trish replies. "But still, they are my priorities, and if I can avoid a broken family at any cost, I will. Plus, you know I take my vows seriously, and I really should look at the bright side—at least Roy still takes me out on dates once in a while. No one is perfect. I just try to focus on the positives in my life."

"I know, Trish. If only I were more like you."

"There's always room in my van on Sundays," Trish says happily, nudging her shoulder against mine.

"One of these days," I reply.

"So, anyway, what are you going to do?"

"What do you mean?"

"You know what I mean. Who are you going to pick? Ethan or Lee?"

"I don't know. Who do you think I should pick?"

Trish smirks. "I think you know who I'd pick, but that doesn't matter. What matters is who makes *you* the most happy."

"That's no help."

"Well, think about it. Who do you see yourself having kids with? Which guy can you picture yourself snuggled up with on the couch at night? Who can you picture yourself growing old with?"

"I don't know. Both," I reply. "Lee is, well, Lee. He has always been my best friend. He knows everything there is to know about me, but Ethan is everything I've always thought I wanted in a husband. Ethan treats me good. I feel like his first priority in life."

Then I remember what Lee said to me before he left me alone in the hotel room. I sigh, "Although, if you would've heard what Lee said when I told him I hadn't broken it off with Ethan, you would think Lee wouldn't be a possible option anymore. I don't think Lee will ever forgive me now."

"Please! Lee's put in so much time and effort waiting for you, I doubt he would give up on you."

"He sounded pretty convincing," I reply.

Trish slaps my thigh a little harder than I would've preferred. "Well, it's not like you need to decide right this second," Trish says and finishes off the bottle.

"Well, good thing you drank ninety-nine percent of that, or I wouldn't be able to take care of your kids for you, would I?" I ask Trish.

Trish smirks.

"Now, I'm starting to think this was your plan all along."

Trish slaps my thigh again and stands up to corral her kids. "Time to head back, kiddos!" she yells. "Auntie wants to play board games with you two while mommy goes to sleep."

"It's barely 4:00, and don't you need to feed them?"

"Oh, yeah… good idea. I had forgotten, with my tummy full of wine and all."

I laugh at Trish's forgetfulness, but I don't blame her. Her schedule is off today, and she's not used to getting a break from her duties as a wife and a mother. I could never judge her. I know she's the best wife and mom anyone could hope for, and like she mentioned, no one's perfect, and no one can deny Trish's genuine love for her family. My sister deserves this break even if she's not actually drunk.

"I'll order a pizza for them," I suggest.

"You are the bestest sister ever," Trish says.

"Bestest?"

"Zoe!" Trish yells, annoyed I'm still not playing along with her boozy night. "I'm kind of drunk!"

A passerby hears Trish. Unfortunately, the lady doesn't know what's really in the bottle and thinks Trish is harming her unborn baby. The lady, who is taking a late-night stroll, shakes her head and makes a comment about how Trish is a bad mother.

"It's a mocktail!" Trish yells, but the lady is too far away. "We're only pretending I'm drunk."

"Does this mean we can stop pretending now?"

"I guess," Trish says, disappointed, and angrily throws the bottle back into her bag before slinging it over her shoulder. "But I still want to fall asleep before the sun sets."

"So, about the board games. Where am I supposed to get my hands on those?"

Trish pats the bag and winks at me.

"Ah, I should've known," I reply.

It didn't take long for Trish to pass out on the hotel bed. She almost stayed awake long enough for pizza—almost. Being a wife and a mom is tiring business.

While Ashley, Travis, and I stuffed our faces with dinner, I constantly checked my phone, not wanting to miss Ethan's call. I'd rather not upset Ethan for another consecutive night in a row, but he ended up not calling during dinner. In fact, Ethan didn't call during our intense hour of board games either.

After I tucked Ashely and Travis in next to their mom, I decided to give Ethan a call since I hadn't heard from him all night. To my surprise, he didn't answer. I figured he must've gotten caught up in some documentary and had his phone on silent or something. No big deal. It was better I didn't have to chat with Ethan with Lee on my mind.

It's getting late, and I'm exhausted from not getting much sleep the night before as well as giving my sister a break. I lie down on the couch and close my eyes, but it's no use, I can't fall asleep. Lee kissing me, Lee's body against mine in the shower, and moments on the hotel bed with him keep replaying in my head. "Stop," I say to myself, more specifically, to my brain. It does as I say, and I stop thinking about the other night, but now past memories are put on a movie reel and begin projecting in my mind. I see Lee and me sitting on the lunch bench years ago, and he's sharing his amazing food with me. A clip of us sitting and laughing in the treehouse is playing, and then a scene from the yogurt shop a couple of years later. Lee takes a spoonful of my yogurt and quickly shoves it into his mouth. I yell at him for stealing my yogurt, and we both are having the best time.

I let the memories flow through my mind, and it helps me drift off. Now, I think I'm starting to dream as the real memories fade. The dream feels like real life. It reminds me of the same dream I had weeks ago, but I wasn't able to stay asleep long enough to see what else happened. It's still only showing Lee and me from the chest up. Maybe this *is* a continuation of my previous dream. I hope it is, but the home we are in isn't Ethan's.

It's Lee's and mine. The background noise is still the same until I hear Lee speak.

"I got you your favorite," Lee says happily.

It isn't until now I can see more than just our faces. My dream pans out, and I see that my stomach is round, and my whole body aches from pregnancy pains—but in a good way, if there is such a thing.

Lee hands me the largest yogurt I've ever seen. "You read my mind," I reply.

Lee sits down beside me and leans over to kiss my belly, and whispers, "I love you, and I can't wait to meet you."

Everything is perfect. Everything is how it should—

I feel my body being shaken back and forth. "Wake up!"

Trish has interrupted my dream. I abruptly sit up as Trish places her hand on her hip in frustration.

"I've been standing here, trying to wake you up for the last minute and a half."

I rub my tired eyes. "It's not like I was able to go to bed while the sun was still partially up like *someone*," I state.

"Oh, whatever," Trish says.

I look at the clock on the hotel nightstand. It's just barely past 6:00 AM. "What the heck? Why are you waking me up at the butt crack of dawn?" I respond irritably.

"Someone's here to see you," Trish says.

I perk up and look around, assuming it's Lee. Maybe he just needed some time to think things over too.

"I made him wait outside," Trish says. "Wasn't sure you wanted to be surprised… well, *more* surprised…"

I quickly stand up and push Trish aside to open the door. As I turn the knob, I start my apology in hopes to make amends. "Lee, I'm so glad you came back. I want to let you know—" Once the door is fully open, I realize it's not who I thought it was.

"*Heyyy*," Ethan says, holding a suitcase. "Surprise…"

My eyes widen as I think back to how loudly I was talking a few seconds ago. Maybe Ethan didn't hear me through the half-opened door.

"Hi there," I reply awkwardly. I lean over and give Ethan a hug.

"You were expecting Lee?" Ethan asks as he steps into the room and places his suitcase on the floor.

"Um—" I stall and look helplessly at Trish.

Trish looks uncomfortable too and claps her hands a couple of times and says, "Okay, children, time to go." She grabs her bag and scoops up the two sleepy children in her arms. "I think Auntie and Ethan need some *alone* time," she rambles like a broken record playing too fast. "I'll see you tomorrow! Okay, bye!"

Trish is out the door before I know it.

I realize my hair is in a ratty bedhead side braid. Even worse, I realize Ethan heard me greet him as Lee, and now I'm quickly pulling out my hair tie and undoing my braid, trying to look more presentable for Ethan.

"Is this why you didn't call last night?" I ask, hoping to revert Ethan from the subject of Lee. "I was waiting up to talk to you. I even tried calling you before I went to bed."

"Oh, yeah. I was busy packing," Ethan explains. "I was able to take some time off of work to join you." Ethan is still standing by his suitcase—purposely keeping himself at a distance since I've taken a seat on the couch. "I missed you," he says, looking like a sad puppy dog.

"I missed you too," I say, but I know my words have less meaning than Ethan's.

"Did you?" Ethan scoffs. "You thought I was Lee. Seems like you haven't been missing me that much."

I purse my lips and grab the pillow off the couch to press against my chest for comfort.

"Should I have stayed home?" Ethan asks sadly.

I shrug and don't make eye contact. "I—I… I'm glad you came," I stammer.

Ethan walks over to me and kneels in front of me. He grabs my hands and looks up at me. "Is there something going on between you and Lee? I desperately want the answer to be no, but you have to be honest with me."

I slide my hands away from his hand, place them over my mouth, not wanting to admit what's been going on with Lee.

"If you tell me nothing has happened, I will believe you, and we can move on with our lives," Ethan says.

So, technically I could lie and tell Ethan that Lee and I never kissed. I could tell him Lee didn't make love to me on the bed I'm staring at right now. I could fabricate an entire story, and Ethan would still marry me. Lee may never give me another chance. I could be alone forever if I'm honest with Ethan, or I could have my happy ending if Ethan never finds out about Lee and me.

Although the devil sitting on my shoulder is persuasive, so is the little guy with wings hanging out on the top of my other shoulder. The one with the halo is telling me a relationship based on lies isn't healthy. He's saying how it wouldn't be fair to Ethan. Ethan's been loyal through and through. Ethan has tried to give you the world and deserves the truth.

"Ethan… I'm so sorry," I say, trying not to cry. "I cheated on you… with Lee."

Ethan's head drops low, and he starts to nod his head. "I figured," he murmurs.

"You don't deserve what I did to you," I say, sliding off the ring Ethan had given me. I grab his hand and open it to place the ring in his palm. "I do love you, and I truly thought I wanted to spend the rest of my life with you, but I—"

"No, I understand," Ethan says, interrupting me. "Deep down, I knew you two had feelings for one another, but I thought I could change your mind. I thought you would choose me, but I was a fool."

"I'm so sorry, Ethan," I whisper. "I didn't intend for this to happen."

Ethan stands up but not completely defeated. He puffs out his chest slightly like he's putting on a façade.

"I guess you can't tell your heart who to love, right?" he chuckles, trying to hide the hurt.

If I smashed Ethan's heart into a million pieces, no one would be able to tell. That's okay, I'd rather see him leave like this. Ethan nods his head again before quickly grabbing his suitcase.

"I mean, I—I know everything is a—"

Ethan interrupts, "Lee's a lucky guy to hold your heart, Zoe."

And before I can get another word in, Ethan is gone just as fast as Trish.

Chapter Ten

Last Chance

I stand in front of Lee's house, hoping I don't get the same answer the last ten times I was here. Okay, ten times might be an exaggeration, but the last handful of times I tried to talk to Lee by ambushing him at his parents' house got me nowhere. His mom ended up making up any excuse not to let me in. She stood at the door like Lee's bodyguard, which I guess I understood the reasoning behind wanting to protect Lee. I'd be upset, too, if someone crushed my little boy's heart.

I feel nervous as I ring the doorbell. I was always welcomed with open arms by Lee's family, heck, I was part of the family up until I brought Ethan into the picture. I desperately hope this time is different.

"Zoe," Mrs. Smith says, not expecting me at her front door.

"Hi," I murmur, waving awkwardly.

She wipes her hands on the apron she's wearing. "Does Bruce know you were stopping by?" she asks hesitantly.

"No," I reply and quickly say something else before she "shoos" me away. "But I have something really important to tell him," I say urgently.

Lee's mom looks unsure if she should allow me to see Lee. Mrs. Smith would make an awesome addition to the Queen's guard if she weren't a tiny Asian woman.

"I promise I won't upset Lee. I have good news," I plead.

Mrs. Smith slowly steps to the side and waves her arm, directing me. "Okay," she says but starts to shake her finger at me. "But you better make things right with Lee. Just when I thought my son was getting over you, you come back to San Diego and stir things up again." I don't dare take a step inside her house until she's done scolding me. "You two have been at the hip too long to just end your friendship… or whatever you want to call your relationship, and you should know by now that I'm too busy cooking to be the middle-man."

"Yes, I know," I say quietly, submitting to Lee's mom. "I'm sorry. I know I've made a lot of mistakes, but I—I… do love your son."

Mrs. Smith finally relaxes and smiles. "I know you do," she replies. "Well, what are you waiting for? Come on in. Last time I checked, Lee was in the treehouse."

Treehouse? Why would Lee be in there? I thank Mrs. Smith and let her return to her steamy kitchen, and I head outside.

The treehouse is just how I remembered it. I had a hard time imagining how Lee managed to get through the door. It had to have been a good fifteen years since we'd last been inside that old thing. I'm surprised his parents haven't demolished it by now to make more room for Mrs. Smith's garden.

I take a deep breath, walk over to the treehouse, and bend over to make my way through the door. As I try to walk hunched over, I trip through the doorway and fall onto Lee's lap.

Lee holds out his hands and reaches for me to break my fall. "Zoe?" Lee asks, shocked. "What are you doing here?"

There's barely enough room for just Lee in here. I shimmy my way over to the other side of the treehouse and sit down, facing him with my knees scrunched against my chest.

"Hi," I say awkwardly.

"What are you doing here?" Lee asks again.

He doesn't necessarily look enthralled to see me. Lee looks like that one time he had to flush his dead fish, Kyle, down the toilet after he overfed him.

"I should ask you the same thing," I chuckle, referring to Lee's choice of cramped space. "Don't you feel a little claustrophobic in here?" I joke.

Lee shrugs, breaks eye contact with me, and looks over his shoulder, literally giving me the cold shoulder.

I look around the inside of the treehouse. "Wow," I laugh and run my fingers over my favorite carving. "Remember when we did this?" I ask.

Lee's demeanor is the same, but I get a little nod out of him.

"I really miss those days," I say. "We had some good times… minus the day I panicked and sprained my pinky."

Lee tries to hide a smirk.

I look at Lee and say, "I'm sorry I hurt you."

He nods a second time but remains speechless.

"I'm sorry I left you for Ethan," I say.

The longer this goes on, the less positive I feel about making amends. If only I can get Lee to talk to me.

"Hey," I say as I run my hand down my hair. "You probably didn't notice, but I decided to go back to my classic side braid, and I got rid of those contacts. It really freaked me out having to touch my eyeball anyway."

"What? Ethan have a change of heart and wanted you to go back to the *original* you?" Lee asks mockingly.

"No, I realized that someone in my life has always loved me, even with my frizzy side braid and oversized glasses."

Lee finally looks at me.

I place my hand on Lee's and continue, "I realized I shouldn't have to change myself for anyone. That's not real love."

Lee looks down at my hand I placed on top of his. "Where's your ring?" he asks, and I no longer see a saddened expression on Lee's face.

"I… gave it back to Ethan," I say proudly.

"Wasn't big enough? Told him to take it back and get a bigger rock?" Lee jokes.

I slap his arm. "Shut it," I reply. "I called off the engagement and broke up with him, and I told him about us—not in that order… of course."

"Of course…" Lee says, slightly chuckling.

"I know I screwed up a lot this last year—"

"Uh-huh," Lee responds.

I glare at him. "Would you let me finish?"

Lee leans back onto the treehouse, causing the old structure to shift slightly and creak.

"I know I messed up a lot the past year, and I guess everyone but me knew you had feelings for me. I'm not really sure how I didn't figure it out. I've always loved you as a friend, but now I know I love you more than just that." I start to talk too fast because I'm not sure what to expect. I hope Lee will give me another chance. "Like, I love, love you, and not just like a friend. I agree you and I are meant—"

"Would you just shut up already," Lee says.

I stop rambling and feel my heart start to race. My palms become clammy, thinking of how I shouldn't have come. I've hurt Lee beyond mending.

"I'm—I'm sorry," I say and try to push myself in an upward position to exit the treehouse.

"What are you sorry for? Sorry that you haven't kissed me already?" Lee asks.

"What?" I ask, confused.

Lee answers my question by placing his hand behind my neck. He forcefully pulls me in and puts his lips on mine.

Lee bonks his head on the roof of the treehouse as he tries to position himself over me, and we can't help but let out a little laugh while Lee unbuttons my shorts.

"I don't think this treehouse is going to make it if we are about to do what we did the other day in the hotel room," I mention.

"It will be fine," Lee says while kissing my neck. "But we should probably think about getting a bigger place."

I place my hand on Lee's chest and push him back just a little, so I can look at him. "You mean, like, a place of our own… together?"

"Yeah, why not?" Lee asks. "You think it's too soon? I know we've only known each other for a short amount of time," he says in a serious tone. "I don't want you to freak out when you realize I forget to double flush."

"Holy cow," I laugh. "But double flushing is a dealbreaker."

"Then I guess I will have to make sure I remember," Lee says, smiling.

"You better," I say. "I really want to get a place with you. That would be perfect."

"Me too," he says and continues where he left off.

"Bao is ready!" Lee's mom screams from the house.

"I am kind of hungry," I say.

"Ugh! Really?" Lee asks, frustrated.

"I'm pretty hungry for some bao, but not as hungry as I am for you," I laugh.

Chapter Eleven

Happy Ending

No! not that kind of "happy ending." Sheesh, get your mind out of the gutter. This happy ending isn't like the ones you find in a fairy tale. It's better because it's the kind of happy ending you find in real life.

With all the money Lee was able to save up while staying with his parents, we were able to purchase a little house, and when I say little, I mean, it's not much bigger than the studio I rented. Also, when we purchased the house, the fence was barely standing, the paint was peeling off the walls, there was this bright red-orange shag carpet, and the backyard consisted of various piles of dirt. I'm sure many buyers tucked their tail and ran once they stepped foot into that house, but Lee and I knew what kind of potential there was behind the cracked paint and thirty-year-old carpet.

After getting settled into our new place, I convinced Lee to follow his dream and open his own gym. Actually, when I rediscovered my "boob jar" fund that I shoved in the back of our closet, I decided it should go toward something that would benefit Lee, you know, to make up for all the yogurt he's bought me over the years… and so much more. Turns out, gym equipment is crazy expensive, much more than a boob job. I was only able to pitch in a little financially, but I was determined to help in other ways.

Luckily for Lee and me, Ethan sent the old yogurt machine back with all my stuff. I'm assuming having it in his kitchen was like rubbing salt into a wound. I've perfected some pretty great yogurt recipes. I've been able to crank out better quality yogurt, which is, surprisingly, low-calorie. Lee couldn't justify feeding his clients an overly sugary treat packed with unnecessary calories or something like that.

So, even though it was a rough path to get where I'm at now—I'm glad I shed those tears, lost myself temporarily, and felt that hurt… because if I never experienced uncertainty and heartache, I wouldn't be where I'm at now. I wouldn't be standing here with my hair in the perfect side braid and glasses on, making yogurt for the love of my life after a long day of work.

Lee locks the doors to the gym and sits down with me to share our favorite treat.

"I love you," he says.

"And *I* love you too," I reply.

If it weren't for my best friend, I might've never been as happy as I am right now. If it weren't for Lee, I might've never realized I am enough.

The most important thing I've learned on my journey so far is to love yourself and don't let anyone change that. If someone doesn't like who you are or what you look like, there's someone out there who will. There's someone in the world who wouldn't change a thing about you because that version of you is perfect.

You. Are. Perfect.

This is, for sure, my happily-ever-after, and I am Lee's perfect girl, but I guess I always have been.

"Want to go home and watch *Twilight?*" I ask.

I've never been so content in all my life when the love of my life replies, "You just read my mind."

The End

Thanks for reading my novel!

I would like to take the opportunity to thank you for your purchase. The support of each reader means everything to me. I hope you fell in love with Zoe and all the characters who surrounded her. If you enjoyed my novel, don't forget to leave a review. I would love to hear from you! Keep in touch with me on social media—where you can learn more about giveaways, discounts, and future novels. I hope to chat with you soon!

Follow me on: Facebook and Instagram
@leahghermann

www.ingramcontent.com/pod-product-compliance
Lightning Source LLC
Chambersburg PA
CBHW061619190726
48288CB00007B/2384

* 9 7 8 1 7 3 7 9 6 7 7 2 9 *